The CONJURERS

HUNT FOR THE LOST

ALSO BY BRIAN ANDERSON

The Conjurers #1: Rise of the Shadow

The CONJURERS

HUNT FOR THE LOST

BOOK TWO

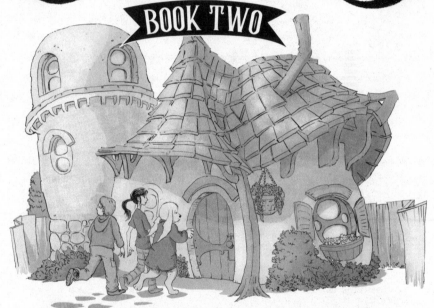

BRIAN ANDERSON

CROWN BOOKS FOR YOUNG READERS

NEW YORK

Visit us on the Web! rhcbooks.com

Educators and librarians, for a variety of teaching tools, visit us at RHTeachersLibrarians.com

Library of Congress Cataloging-in-Publication Data
Names: Anderson, Brian, author.
Title: Hunt for the lost / Brian Anderson.
Description: First edition. | New York: Crown Books for Young Readers, [2021] | Series: The conjurers; [#2] | Audience: Ages 8–12. | Audience: Grades 4–6. | Summary: "Siblings Alex and Emma are back in the Conjurian world where the race to find the Eye of Dedi and save all magic is on! But the hunt gets even more dangerous at every turn."—Provided by publisher.
Identifiers: LCCN 2020009447 (print) | LCCN 2020009448 (ebook) |
ISBN 978-0-553-49869-1 (hardcover) | ISBN 978-0-553-49870-7 (library binding) |
ISBN 978-0-553-49872-1 (trade paperback) | ISBN 978-0-553-49871-4 (ebook)
Subjects: CYAC: Magic—Fiction. | Brothers and sisters—Fiction. | Rabbits—Fiction. | Fantasy.
Classification: LCC PZ7.A5228 Hun 2020 (print) | LCC PZ7.A5228 (ebook) | DDC [E]—dc23

Printed in the United States of America
10 9 8 7 6 5 4 3 2 1
First Edition

*For all my teachers at St. John's High School
in Shrewsbury, Massachusetts. Especially Mr. Lahey,
Mr. Jourcin, Mrs. Curran, and Mr. Dolan. Although I had
no idea at the time, you gave me all the tools I would need
to pull off the impossible. That is true magic. Thank you.*

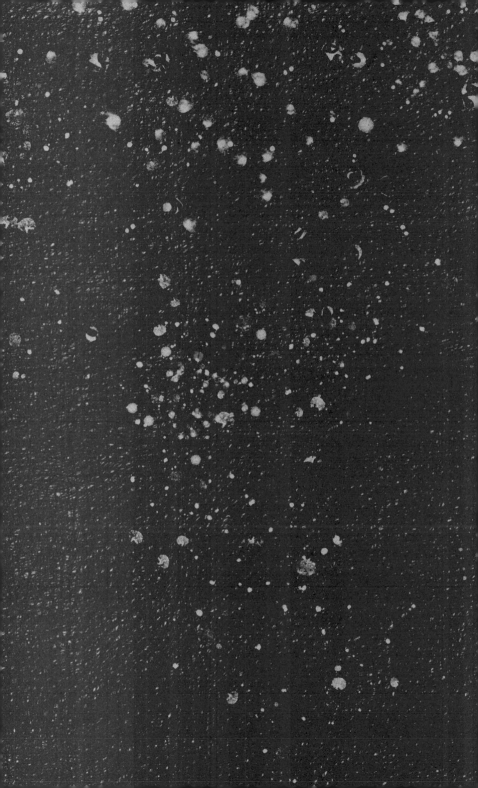

CHAPTER 1

EMMA

I'm blind, thought Emma, instinctively rubbing her eyes. She opened and closed them.

No difference. This was not good.

She detected damp earth, tasting it, crunching it between her teeth. Every breath scratched her throat.

She tried calling to the others, but no sound escaped her grime-coated mouth.

I'm buried alive!

Panic crept through her. What had happened? She remembered Clive Grubian picking her up and carrying her under one enormous arm—his brother, Neil, under the other—as the Conjurian Detention Center shook around them. The boy, Savachia, had been behind them, dragging his father. Then Clive had let her fall and collapsed on top of her, a second before a wave of dirt exploded down the corridor, destroying all light and sound.

Clive had saved her. If you counted being buried alive as safe. But she couldn't see. She couldn't move.

And what about her brother? What about Alex?

She'd bluffed her way into this prison to find and rescue Alex. But she hadn't been able to locate him. Had he been locked in one of the cells? Had he been crushed when the earthquake hit?

Did that mean Emma had been left completely alone? No family at all?

Something grunted and moved above her, and suddenly Emma could breathe more easily. A hand seized her arm and pulled her up through a few inches of loose dirt, and she was standing in the corridor, coughing and gasping.

"Neil? Clive?" she sputtered.

"I hope they're crushed under the debris," muttered an irritated voice—Savachia's. He coughed. "Some help they turned out to be."

"Neil!" Emma called again, ignoring the boy.

Sparks flickered before her eyes. Then Neil's face, round as the moon, appeared in front of her, lit by a flame dancing on the tip of his thumb.

"You're alive!" Emma beamed with relief. She barely knew the two Grubian brothers, but in the relief of knowing that she was not all alone in the dark, she could have hugged the short, rotund Neil and his gigantic brother, Clive, visible now as the flame on Neil's thumb grew bigger and brighter.

Clive nodded at Emma and returned to his task. He was industriously stuffing tiny sacks into small cracks in the wooden wall of the prison.

Emma looked up and down the corridor, but she could not look far. The ceiling to her right had caved in, blocking the hallway completely. To her left, the passage was choked with dirt. Emma could see no sign of Sergeant Miller or his men, who had been just about to arrest every single one of them.

Savachia crouched by his father's limp body. He'd finagled his way into this prison, along with Emma, in order to rescue his father—but he hadn't told her about his plan. She had thought he'd been here to help her rescue Alex.

She'd been wrong. About that. About a lot of things.

Emma reached out to tug on Neil's soiled jacket. "There's no way out. We're buried alive!"

"Now, my dear, we are not buried. Although we are alive. Details count." Neil nodded at his flaming thumb. Emma's grip on his jacket threatened to pull his coat sleeve down over his hand, smothering the flame.

Emma quickly removed her hand.

"You have to have faith," said Neil. "Do you trust me?"

Emma hesitated.

No. The answer was no. She'd only just met the Grubian brothers, shortly after flying skeletons called Rag-O-Rocs had invaded the mansion that belonged to Emma's uncle. Uncle Mordo had shouted at Emma and Alex to run, to save themselves, to follow Emma's pet rabbit, Pimawa. And they had.

Pimawa had turned out to be more than a pet. He was actually a Jimjarian, a walking, talking servant bound to serve a magician all his life. He'd brought them to the Conjurian, into the Mysts, where they were attacked by an entirely different kind of monster, a bandiloc. It had been Neil and Clive Grubian who'd saved them from the bandiloc and who'd taken Emma and Alex and Pimawa to Conjurian City.

Emma had thought they'd be safe there. That was one of the many things she'd been wrong about.

Conjurian City was where Emma had been kidnapped (by Savachia), where her brother, Alex, had been taken prisoner (by their uncle's old colleague Christopher Agglar), and where Emma had been told by the man who had been her dead parents' closest friend that he would not help her or protect her.

Conjurian City was where Emma had learned to trust no one at all.

But she had no choice now. She could not get herself out of this prison, where the collapsed roof and crushed walls and tons of dirt trapped her and the others more securely than locks and bars.

If Neil had a way out, she *had* to trust him.

She met his eyes and nodded.

Neil held the flame closer to Clive, who stuffed one last pouch into a small crevice and stepped back.

Emma had seen pouches like that before, in the Grubians' carriage. They had been full of woofle seeds. Emma didn't know much about woofle seeds, but she knew that they could explode.

Hope blossomed inside her, bright as Neil's flame. They weren't buried alive after all—or they wouldn't be for long!

Clive stepped back and spread his great arms, gesturing for all of them to step behind him. Emma did so quickly, nodding at Savachia to do the same. He was a liar and a traitor, and she would be sure to tell him exactly what she thought of him once they were free—but that didn't mean she wanted to see him blown up.

Savachia dragged his father behind Clive as the larger of the two Grubian brothers kicked the wall hard. Nothing happened.

"Kick harder, you elongated barber pole!" shouted Neil.

Clive kicked repeatedly.

"For the love of—move aside and let me—" Neil

squirmed out from behind Clive just as the woofle seeds erupted in a blinding, golden flash. The tough wooden roots that made up the walls of the Conjurian Detention Center were wrenched apart, and the earth that surrounded them shuddered and split, revealing a slender fissure. Fresh air washed in.

"Ladies first." Neil coughed. He helped Emma into the crack. "When

we get to the carriage," he added, jabbing a finger into his brother's gut, "you will spend the rest of the day checking the expiration dates on all the woofle seeds."

Emma clawed her way up, emerging into the giant field that lay at the foot of the Tower of Dedi. She looked around, hoping beyond hope to see Alex rushing toward her.

Instead she was enveloped in a curtain of sooty air. Chunks of wall and piles of brick and stone littered the plain and choked the gaps between the roots. She clambered up onto an arching root, desperately searching for the Tower of Dedi through the filthy air.

"Miss Emma!" croaked Neil, climbing out after her, followed by his brother. "We should stay low until the air clears." Rasping, Neil leaned against the root Emma was standing on. "Come down before someone, or something, spots you!"

A wind gust briefly cleared the murky sky, and Emma gasped. There, not more than two hundred yards away, stood what remained of the Tower of Dedi.

The last time Emma had been aboveground, the Tower had risen over this plain like a skyscraper. It was a building created out of the largest living tree Emma had ever seen. It made a California redwood look like a spindly sapling.

And now it had fallen.

That was what had caused the cave-in, Emma realized. Not an earthquake. The Tower had collapsed.

Only the stump of the tree remained. The few surviving branches curled downward like the hands of a corpse.

"It's gone," said Emma.

Neil jerked his head up. Clive straightened up to stare. Savachia, tugging his father's body with him, was last to reach the surface. Even he seemed dumbstruck.

"My brother was in there," said Emma. "My brother was in the Tower!" She glared down at Savachia. "If you had done what you promised, he'd be alive!"

First Savachia had kidnapped Emma to use as a hostage. Then, after she'd begged and bargained, he'd agreed to help her sneak into the Tower to find Alex. But he hadn't done that. Instead he'd used her to get inside the Tower and then left her on her own while he went off to rescue his father.

Now, after one glance at the Tower, Savachia sat down in the dirt, bending over his father's motionless form.

"Now, now," said Neil, patting Emma's shoe. "I am sure a boy as clever as Alex found a way out. In fact, it is entirely possible he is responsible for the destruction we see before us. Probably took out Christopher Agglar and his henchmen in one go. The head of the Circle stood no chance against a boy as resourceful as your brother."

Emma stabbed her finger back toward the space where the Tower once stood. "No one got out of that! He's gone!" Her foot slipped.

Clive reached her in one stride. He wrapped his arms around her waist and lowered her gently to the ground.

Neil took her hand in his, patting it. "We made it out. Didn't we? And I daresay your brother is cleverer than the lot of us together."

Emma flung Neil's hand away, glaring down at Savachia.

His back to her, he sat hunched over his father. It was as if he could not hear her.

Emma's fists were clenched so tightly that her fingernails cut into her palms. "This is your fault! I should never have trusted you!" she yelled at Savachia. "You're nothing more than a con artist! A no-good thief!"

Savachia shrugged. He got to his feet and walked a few steps away from his father, from Emma, from Neil and Clive. He stood with his back to them, looking at the devastation that surrounded them.

"Answer me!" Emma screamed at him.

He shrugged again, without turning.

"Ah, my dear Jane. Emma. Perhaps you might—" Neil ventured.

Emma ignored him. "What's the matter with you?" she demanded of Savachia.

"He's dead," Savachia said without looking at her.

Emma's breath and her words rushed out of her. She knew it. She knew Alex was gone. But to hear it like that, said so simply and brutally—it made her want to crumple to the ground.

Then she realized that Savachia was not talking about Alex at all.

Her eyes fell on the boy's father, lying faceup on the ground. The man didn't look much like Savachia. He was thin—well, he'd been in prison a long time. They didn't feed you all that well, probably. His hair and beard were disheveled. His eyes were closed, and his face was white. So white.

Of course, he'd been shut up in a cell away from the sun.

Likely for a long time. But this kind of whiteness and stillness—Emma knew it could only mean one thing.

"Smothered, probably," said Savachia, still staring away. "Or a heart attack, maybe, when all that dirt came down over us. He wasn't strong. He'd been in that place so long."

Emma stared.

Her anger still sputtered and flared inside her, but how could she shriek at Savachia now? How could she batter at him with her fists or demand that he—what? Apologize? Fix what he'd done?

No apology could help. There was nothing to fix. Alex was dead. Just like Savachia's father was dead.

Neil cleared his throat.

"A tragedy indeed. My most sincere condolences. But now, my dears, we must figure out our next move."

Next move? A pain like no other, a hollow ache, filled Emma from head to toe. She had nothing left. No parents. No uncle. No brother. No home. She watched as Savachia pressed a kiss to his father's temple, then laid him on the dirt. What she was sure would be his final resting place.

Suddenly, Emma realized she had something after all, something new filling the void, replacing the ache: revenge.

"I know what the next move is," said Emma. "I find the Shadow Conjurer and make him pay."

It was the Shadow Conjurer who'd sent the Rag-O-Rocs to kill Uncle Mordo. It was the Shadow Conjurer who'd chased Emma and Alex into the Conjurian, a magical world where magic was slowly dying. It was the Shadow Conjurer's fault that Emma had lost everyone she'd ever loved.

"Well, okay, that was specific," said Neil, taken aback. Suddenly he looked up at a shadow winding through the brackish sky toward them. "Rag-O-Roc! Run!"

"Let it come!" Emma shoved Clive aside and clambered back onto the root. Her teeth were clenched so tight she thought they might shatter. Her fists shook at her sides. The growing anger had given her power, and she liked it.

Clive attempted to bear-hug her legs. Emma hopped sideways out of his reach. No one was stopping her now! She wasn't going to run. Glowering at the beast on its collision course, she noticed something familiar. "It's not a Rag-O-Roc," she said, startled. "It's—"

The creature spiraled into Emma, sending them both crashing to the ground. "Geller!" Emma cradled the rumpled parrot. "What are you doing here?"

"I came to fetch my master after Master Agglar's thugs abducted him." Geller removed his cracked glasses, wiped them on his feathers, and balanced them back on his beak.

"Agglar's people took Derren?" Emma asked. She remembered how she'd last seen Derren Fallow—her parents' oldest friend—holding off Sergeant Miller, giving her time to flee with Savachia.

Derren had let her down. She'd gone to him for help, and he hadn't done a thing. But then he'd put himself at risk to let her escape.

So Derren had been arrested? Had he been inside the Tower too?

Geller flapped the dust from his wings. "Yes, indeed. But my master made it out. With the boy and the Jimjarian. I am afraid I lost them when the Tower fell."

Emma was glad she was already sitting on the ground, or she was sure she would have fallen over. *The boy.* Geller had said *the boy.* Did he mean . . . "Alex? Was Alex with Derren? And Pimawa? They're . . ." She had to stop to breathe. "Alive?"

"Certainly they were." Geller looked almost offended. "You don't think a trifle like a falling tower could have stopped my master, do you?"

Emma wanted to hug Geller—glasses, snooty look, and all. "Which way? Where were they headed?" she asked.

Geller scowled at her through the cracked lenses of his spectacles. "Toward the water."

Emma stood, placing Geller on a root. "Can you show us the way?" she asked eagerly.

Geller gingerly tested one wing. "It would appear I'm grounded for the time being. And it would take ages to climb through this debris."

"Well, taddely toophers, I'm not much of a climber," Neil said. He clapped his hands to his chest, choking on the grime that wafted from his jacket, and removed a small black box with a red button from an inside pocket. He pushed the button. A sharp double beep answered in the distance. "But I always have an escape plan from my escape plan."

click!

CHAPTER 2

ALEX

Alex felt himself floating gently downward. The pain in his chest, like a vise tightening moment by moment, was fierce but somehow far away.

The water was getting darker around him. Or maybe his eyes were closing. He wasn't sure.

He didn't really care.

He'd plunged into the river to avoid the Rag-O-Rocs. He'd been fleeing from them, trying to lead them away from Derren and Pimawa and Pimawa's father, Rowlfin. He hoped the three of them had gotten safely away. If they had, they could find Emma. Save Emma.

It was probably too late for anybody to save Alex.

He felt his body settle onto something solid. The darkness closed in. He didn't notice when the surface he was lying on began to rise gently, carrying him up toward the surface of the water—and the Rag-O-Rocs.

His limp body broke the surface of the water. There was a thump, and whatever he was lying on shook. Dimly, he heard a far-off voice. "Master Alex! Master Alex, please be alive. Please!"

"Hold on to him, Pimawa!"

"What about those creatures? Master Fallow, where are they?" Pimawa's voice was tense.

"The Rag-O-Rocs are flying away," Derren answered grimly. "What *is* that thing? What is he lying on?"

A squeal of metal grating on metal pierced Alex's ears.

"Ahoy!" a cheerful voice shouted.

Neil? Could that be Neil Grubian? Surely not. Alex lay still without opening his eyes and decided that he must be delirious. He was dying and his brain was bringing up random images from his past. Although why one of the Grubian brothers should be included in those visions he could not imagine.

He'd last seen Neil and Clive Grubian in the streets of Conjurian City, being led toward the Tower in chains. Alex had been in exactly the same condition. Neil Grubian could not have ended up in the river, obviously.

Well, Alex had ended up in the river. He had to admit that. But it was way too much of a coincidence for Neil to be there too.

And it was too tiring to worry about right now. Alex felt

his last scrap of consciousness begin to slip away as the voice that sounded exactly like Neil's went on talking.

"Please stop dropping Jimjarians and young lads on our carriage," said Neil. "Maybe it's best if you all come aboard and we get this Maskelyne child resuscitated."

"Is he breathing?"

"Turn him on his side!"

"Everyone, move back. Give Derren some room."

"He's breathing!"

Alex heard the muffled voices. Someone nudged him over, and he tasted river water as it spouted from his mouth.

He opened his eyes. A beaming face grew into focus. "Derren?"

"You're alive!" Emma leaped forward and fell to her knees beside her brother, clutching him hard.

"Emma?" coughed Alex.

Emma softened her grip. "Promise you'll never leave me again. Never, ever again."

He coughed some more. Emma eased him back onto a soggy beanbag chair. He recognized the beanbag. He recognized the room the beanbag was in. He was inside the Grubians' carriage, the one that was pulled by their mechanical alpaca, Gertie.

After the Grubians had driven away the bandiloc, Alex had repaired Gertie and been repaid with a ride to Conjurian City, a place he'd be happy to never see again. In Conjurian City Alex had been separated from his sister, taken prisoner, and very nearly crushed by a falling tower. He'd been chased through the streets by terrifying flying skeletons in fluttering robes and had just about drowned trying to avoid them.

Now he seemed to be back in the carriage, which was rocking gently as it traveled. How had he ended up here? And where was Gertie taking him this time?

"Sorry," Emma said. "It's just that . . . the Tower . . . I thought you were—"

"I know." Alex nodded and reached out to grip his sister's hand. Her face was smeared with dirt, and tears had made clean tracks on her cheeks through the grime. She had on her navy T-shirt, though it was a fair bit dingier than when she'd first put it on. "I thought you were too."

Emma leaned forward and hugged him again, much more gently this time. "We have to stick together. No matter what," she told him.

"Agreed." Alex flopped back against the beanbag. A parrot wearing spectacles flew over him, draping a blanket across his legs. "We ought to get you out of those wet clothes," said the parrot.

"Why is that bird talking?" Alex asked Emma.

"It's Geller," Emma said, as if that were an answer.

"Right. Geller." Alex blinked muddy water out of his eyes and looked around the carriage, which seemed to be full of people. He saw Neil and Clive Grubian. That wasn't surprising, since it was their carriage. He saw Derren and Pimawa and Pimawa's father, Rowlfin, which was a relief. The Rag-O-Rocs had not carried the three of them off. Good.

Then he saw—

"You!" Alex croaked, and he heaved himself up from the beanbag and lunged at Savachia.

Savachia skipped nimbly behind an antique spice rack. Emma grabbed Alex's arm and pulled him back onto the beanbag chair.

"Forget about him," she said.

"He kidnapped you!"

"That doesn't matter anymore." Emma placed her palm on Alex's soaking chest. "We found each other. That's what matters."

"Where did he take you? Did he hurt you?"

"No." Emma wiped droplets off Alex's forehead. "He took me to Derren. Not that *he* was any help."

"What are you talking about?" Alex frowned at his sister. "Derren got us out of the Tower. Pimawa, Rowlfin, and me."

"I bet it was only because his own neck was on the line," Emma said bitterly.

Alex looked across the carriage to see Derren slumped on a box that held a flat-screen TV. He met Alex's eyes but didn't try to defend himself.

"Speaking of saving necks . . ." Savachia looked out from behind the spice rack. "What *did* happen back there, in the Tower?"

"None of your business," snapped Alex.

"Considering that it fell on us," said Neil, "I, for one, would love to hear what transpired."

Alex remembered his last moments in the room at the very top of the Tower. "The Shadow Conjurer came," he said slowly.

Derren shifted uncomfortably on his box, looking away.

"He came for me. I think. But Agglar tried to fight him. He held him off."

"Agglar did that?" Emma was confused. "But I thought . . ." She looked at Derren. He still didn't say a word. "You said Christopher Agglar *was* the Shadow Conjurer," Emma remarked accusingly. "Or was behind him, at any rate. You said he'd made the Shadow Conjurer up to scare people." Christopher Agglar had been the head of the Circle, the council of magicians that ruled the Conjurian. Derren had been a part of the Circle too . . . before he'd quit. "You said if people got scared enough, then they'd let Agglar rule the Conjurian however he wanted."

Derren cleared his throat. "It seems . . . I was mistaken," he said slowly.

Neil shrugged. "To be fair," he said, "a lot of people suspected Agglar was pulling the Shadow Conjurer's strings."

"They were liars and traitors!" Rowlfin burst out. "Master Agglar is dead!"

"What?" said Savachia. Clive Grubian made a startled noise deep in his throat. Neil raised both eyebrows.

"The Shadow Conjurer killed him," Rowlfin went on. "Master Agglar gave his life to save us from that . . . beast." Rowlfin turned, scowling at his son. "After so many doubted him. If people had focused on their duties instead of foolish gossip, the Tower would still stand!"

"Serving blindly is not always the answer," snapped Pimawa. "Master Agglar's sacrifice was noble indeed, but the fact remains—"

"Fact? Fact?" Rowlfin glowered at his son. "It was doubters like you who—"

"Enough!" Derren rose and stepped between the two Jimjarians. "We have all made mistakes." He glanced at Emma and looked away. "But we must admit now that the Shadow Conjurer is real, and that these two children are his target."

"The Eye of Dedi is his target," Alex corrected him. "He just thinks we're the way to get to it. He thinks we know where it is."

"Either way, I say it is high time to hightail it as far away as possible," said Neil. "Clive was just saying how delightful the Banakek Canyons are this time of year."

"I'm tired of being hunted," said Emma. She sat down next to her brother. "Alex and I have been running away since the moment we got to the Conjurian. Since before that! Since the Rag-O-Rocs stormed into Uncle Mordo's mansion and . . . and killed him." She swallowed. "And all that running hasn't accomplished a thing. We have to fight back."

"With what, Emma?" Alex sat up straight in alarm. "We're surrounded by magicians who don't even have enough magic powers to make balloon animals! What chance do we have against an army of skeleton monsters?"

Alex couldn't help a shudder as he remembered the Rag-O-Rocs, faces of pure, bare bone grinning at him through a hole in the roof of the Tower. How did Emma think they were going to fight creatures like that? How did she think they were going to defeat someone with the Shadow Conjurer's powers?

Once, Alex would have scoffed at the idea of anyone having magical powers. But he'd seen the Shadow Conjurer come sailing through the sky toward the Tower of Dedi. He'd seen the man standing on thin air, hundreds of feet above the ground. He'd seen his blue, eyeless face marked by three red scars. And he had very little wish to see any of those things again.

Emma opened her mouth to respond. Instead she grabbed another beanbag, dragged it to the other side of the carriage, and sat, arms crossed.

Alex ran his hand through his wet hair. "Come on, Emma. Think about it. How are we going to fight back against those Rag-O-Rocs? What *are* those things, anyway? Where did they even come from?"

"Ah." Neil snapped his stubby fingers. "That is something we know a little about. Clive, if you would?"

The taller of the two Grubian brothers opened a cabinet on the wall. Inside, a row of marionettes hung limply from a rod.

Alex rolled his eyes. "Can't you just tell us? Without the toys?" The last time he'd seen the Grubians' puppet show, they'd explained the legend of the Eye of Dedi. Dedi was supposed to have created this entire world—the Conjurian—by packing his magical powers inside a pebble that people called his Eye.

Alex had his doubts, but people here sure seemed to believe in this Eye thing. Christopher Agglar certainly had. So did the Shadow Conjurer. And they were pretty much

convinced that Emma and Alex's parents had found the thing (that part might be true) and that therefore Emma and Alex knew where it was (that part definitely wasn't).

"Have a little appreciation for our artistry, young Maskelyne," Neil said cheerfully. Clive picked up a puppet and shook out its strings. A moment later an Egyptian peasant was strolling around the carriage under the control of Clive's huge but deft fingers.

"The legend goes," said Neil, climbing onto the table, "that Dedi used the Eye to create the Conjurian and fled into it, escaping the wrath of the Pharaoh. Then the Pharaoh used every resource at his disposal to discover what he had hoped to learn from Dedi—the secret of restoring life to the deceased. He succeeded. Sort of. The Pharaoh rounded up every magician within five thousand miles. Somehow he drained the magic from his prisoners. The results were not what he intended."

Clive flicked his wrist. The puppet twisted into a wooden caricature of a Rag-O-Roc, which flew around the carriage, grinning with its skull face, snatching with its bony claws.

"So you're saying . . ." Alex let his voice trail away as he thought. "The Rag-O-Rocs used to be people? They used to be magicians? *That's* what happens to a magician when you take his magic away?"

"Indeed." Neil nodded.

"How could the Shadow Conjurer be powerful enough to drain the magic from other magicians and yet remain anonymous?" asked Rowlfin scornfully as he ducked to avoid the puppet.

"That," said Neil, hopping down from the table, "remains in the unsolved column." He clapped his hands, and the puppet landed on his shoulder.

"Regardless of who he is or how he came by his power,

the Shadow Conjurer won't stop until he finds the Eye," said Pimawa. "That is why he is pursuing the children, after all. And why he tore the Tower to shreds."

"But why, exactly?" Alex asked. "I keep hearing how powerful the Eye is and how much everybody wants it. What can it actually do? What is the Shadow Conjurer going to do with it if he ever gets his hands on it?"

Derren spoke up grimly. "The Eye created this world by splitting it off from the Flatworld—the one you grew up in, Alex. And Emma." He glanced at Emma and then away. "I expect that the Shadow Conjurer believes he can use the Eye to join the Conjurian and the Flatworld once again. Essentially, to destroy both worlds and then re-create them as his own. A world he can rule."

"Oh," said Alex. Well, now he knew. "Okay, then. Emma, you were right all along." And there was a sentence he never thought he'd say about his dreamy, impractical sister. "Remember what you said right after we ended up in the Conjurian? We've got to find the Eye. We've got to keep it out of the Shadow Conjurer's hands. We've got to finish what our parents started."

"No." Emma sank back into her beanbag chair.

"Huh?" Alex looked up at her. "What do you mean, no? I'm agreeing with you."

"We're not going to run off on some quest for a pebble. We've got to go after the Shadow Conjurer right now. Build an army, stand up, and fight. We can't waste time running around hunting artifacts."

Alex slumped back in his own beanbag and groaned.

"Miss Emma, I disagree," said Pimawa, shaking his head until his whiskers trembled. "We don't stand a chance."

Rowlfin grunted. "My son, the coward. Master Mordo would be appalled."

"Master Mordo ordered me to keep these children safe." Pimawa's ears lifted slowly until they were fully erect.

Rowlfin clenched his furry paws. "My master died fighting that abomination."

"Look, it's crazy to talk about fighting. Finding the Eye is the key to stopping the Shadow Conjurer," insisted Alex. "We have to go to Plomboria!"

Pimawa's head turned toward him quickly. So did Rowlfin's.

"Plomboria? What are you talking about?" asked Emma. "What is Plomboria?"

Rowlfin stepped between them, eyeing Alex. "Plomboria is home. My home. The home of all Jimjarians. Are you saying that the Eye might be there? How do you know?"

"Yeah, Alex," said Emma. "How *do* you know?"

Alex fished a soggy note from his sweatshirt. He'd found it in his parents' old office in the Tower. It had been hidden behind a picture of a dog he couldn't remember, a family pet that must have been given away when his parents died, the year he turned two.

Pimawa took the note and unfolded it carefully. Alex had memorized the words the Jimjarian must be reading. But the marks of his mother's tears in one corner would have been washed away by the brackish water of the river.

Pimawa read the note aloud.

Dear Alex,

Someday you will go looking for answers.
If you have found this, I'm sure you have a
lot of questions. It also means we failed to
keep you safe. I wish we could be there to tell
you everything. Take your sister to Plomboria.
She's a dreamer. Brave but too trusting.
Keep her safe.

Go now. Trust your instincts. And know
that everything we did was because we love you
and your sister.

Love,
Mom

"I can see why your mother and father would want you to go to Plomboria," he said, nodding. "It's surrounded by water. A secure location. And everyone there is Jimjarian. We have all sworn to serve magicians. No Jimjarian would betray either of you to the Shadow Conjurer. It would be a good place to keep you both safe. But Master Alex, this note says nothing about the Eye's location."

"It doesn't need to," said Alex. "Our parents must have figured that if we somehow ended up finding that hidden note in their office, we were well past the hiding stage. They must have known we'd be looking for the Eye. It makes sense they would leave a trail of clues to its location. They knew that finding the Eye would be our only chance to survive."

"That's ridiculous!" Emma snapped.

CHAPTER 3

EMMA

Emma jumped up from her beanbag chair and snatched the note from Pimawa's paw. A corner of the damp paper tore. She didn't care.

The note was addressed to her brother, not her. Her parents had thought she was a dreamer. Too trusting. They'd thought she would need her little brother to protect her—and they'd written a note to tell him so. They hadn't written anything to her.

What did Henry and Evelynne Maskelyne know about their own daughter? Nothing! They weren't even around to help. They never had been, and that wasn't changing now.

Emma crumpled the note and chucked it at her brother.

She didn't need him—or anyone—to protect her. She was going to fight back, even if she had to do it alone.

While Alex, Neil, Clive, Pimawa, Rowlfin, Derren, and Savachia all stared after her, Emma hurried up the ladder and out the hatch, up onto the carriage's roof. She dropped the hatch closed behind her with an echoing clang.

Near the front of the carriage was a small bench, where a driver might sit if Gertie, the mechanical alpaca, needed to be driven. Right now Gertie was paddling steadily ahead, pulling the carriage behind her, and the bench was empty.

Emma sat on it.

On the left, a barrier of sheer rock scrolled past, the surf crashing against the base. On the right, the ocean spread to meet the sky, now a splotchy pink and violet stained by a dying orange.

After a while, Emma heard the hatch open behind her. She heard it close. She heard footsteps.

Savachia sat down beside her.

"Nice view," he said after a while.

Emma ignored him.

"Your brother keeps glaring at me down there," Savachia said. "I thought it might be more pleasant up here."

Emma ignored him some more.

"I might have been wrong about that, though."

Emma sighed.

"You can't be surprised Alex doesn't like you much," she pointed out. "He thinks you're a kidnapper."

"Well, I am." Savachia looked at her sideways. "And a liar. And a thief. And a con man."

"Is that supposed to make me less mad at you?" Emma asked.

Savachia shrugged. "Up to you, I guess. The point I was going to make is, all that stuff—okay, most of that stuff— I did it to help my dad."

Emma hadn't thought she could feel any worse. And now she did.

"I'm sorry about your father," she said weakly. "I really am."

Savachia nodded.

"I always knew he might not make it," he said quietly, staring at the horizon. "He'd been in those cells a long time."

"Why was he . . . ?" Emma's question faded away. Maybe she didn't have a right to ask.

"He was a thief. Like me. Where do you think I learned it all? He was hunting down magical artifacts."

"So he could sell them? On the black market, that kind of thing?"

Savachia still didn't look at her. "No. So he could find one that would cure my mother."

Emma felt as if something cold and solid and slimy had landed right in the middle of her stomach.

"You said . . . you told me your mom was . . . that she'd died," she protested.

Savachia shrugged. "Yeah. I lie a lot. My mom's not dead. But she's sick. Really sick. Back in the Flatworld. My dad's from here, you know. But he fell in love with my mom on a trip to the Flatworld, and they got married and had me. When she got sick, he tried everything—every doctor, every drug, you name it. Then he came back to the Conjurian to see if he could find something here. He even talked about tracking down the Eye. He figured that would cure her if anything would."

"And then he . . . got arrested?"

Savachia turned to look at her.

"Yeah. By your dad."

Emma froze. "What?"

"It was your father who arrested mine. Ironic, huh? So he got tossed in jail, and I did my best to take care of my mom back home. Then I headed over here to see if I could get him out, somehow. And I did. Too late."

Emma didn't know what to say.

"Look. I'm not telling you all this so you'll feel sorry for me or anything."

"Good. Because I don't," Emma snapped.

Or she tried to snap. It didn't work very well.

What she'd said was a lie. She did feel sorry for Savachia. But the boy had used her for his own purposes more than once, and she needed to be careful. Maybe he was telling her all this precisely so that she *would* feel sorry for him. Maybe that was a feeling he'd use to his own advantage.

Savachia didn't take offense. "I'm just saying, I know what it's like not to have family. And I saw how you were when you thought your brother was gone. He's back now."

Behind them, the hatch clanged open.

"Oh." Savachia looked up. "And he's here, too. Okay. Three's a crowd."

Savachia got up and ducked back down the hatch. Alex stood staring after him.

"What did *he* want?"

Emma sighed. "It's complicated."

Alex sat down next to her. He pulled out a pocket watch from his pants and began fiddling with it, flipping the lid open to glance at the face of the clock inside, snapping it closed again.

It had been their father's watch, Emma knew. "The water didn't hurt it," he offered. "I mean, it didn't break it any more than it was already broken."

"Good," Emma said briefly.

Alex flipped the watch shut for a final time and tucked it into his pocket.

"I wonder how Gertie stays waterproof," he said after a while.

Emma didn't answer.

"If I had a wrench and a screwdriver and a lot of time, I bet I could figure it out. Gertie's pretty cool, but she's just, you know, gears and levers and nuts and bolts. In the end."

Emma still didn't answer. If she stayed quiet long enough, Alex would go away eventually. He always had before.

"Yep. No unsolvable mysteries about Gertie. Em, remember my fifth birthday?" Alex asked.

Emma did. But she certainly didn't want to talk about it. Birthdays? Now? With the world coming to pieces around them and the Shadow Conjurer on their trail?

"You told me that Mom and Dad would come home for my fifth birthday. The supreme tyrant—I mean, sorry, Uncle Mordo—made fried chicken and coleslaw for dinner since he knew that was my favorite." Alex sighed. "I was so mad at him for so long, I kind of forgot how he'd do that on our birthdays. He got me a big present that year too. Remember? All wrapped up with a giant bow?"

Emma remembered.

"I didn't even care," Alex went on. "I sat with you on the stairs waiting for that front door to open. The chicken went cold and I had zero interest in unwrapping my gift, because I believed you. I believed Mom and Dad were going to walk through that door and it would be the best birthday ever."

Emma felt tears stinging in her eyes. When she glanced at Alex, she saw that his own eyes were suspiciously shiny.

"The sun went down, and Uncle Mordo made us go to bed," he said. "You put up a fuss. You were convinced Mom and Dad would show up any minute. But I didn't argue.

I went to bed, Em, because that was the moment I stopped believing. I swore to never believe anything again without evidence to back it up."

Emma pulled her knees up and hugged them tight.

"I believe in facts, Em," said Alex. "We have none. We know nothing about this Shadow Conjurer except that he's ruthless and he's after the Eye of Dedi. Look. We can't rush in blind because we're mad. You want to fight him? Well, we've got to have something to fight him *with*. If the Eye created this world, it's got to be able to help us defend it. And Mom and Dad left us clues about where to find it. If we can get to it before the Shadow Conjurer, we might have a chance. This whole world might have a chance."

Emma put her face against her knees so that Alex wouldn't see her tears falling.

"Em? Please?" He sounded so young, like the little brother who used to cling to her. Who'd trusted her. Who'd believed her when she promised that Mom and Dad were coming back.

"Okay," she said softly. "You're right."

"Whoa. I am?"

Emma picked up her face. "Why so surprised? You always think you're right."

"Yeah, but you don't usually agree."

Emma sniffed and wiped her eyes. "Well, this time I do. And I'm sorry. About your birthday. I'm sorry I told you Mom and Dad were coming back."

Alex nodded. "It's okay. I know you believed it."

Emma didn't believe it anymore.

ALEX

The sun shone through the seawater sloshing against a window, which Alex now realized was actually a porthole. The carriage was cramped and smelled stale, and the Grubians' snoring had kept Alex awake.

He squirmed on his beanbag and something poked him in the butt. Reaching a hand into the back pocket of his cargo pants, he pulled out the book he had taken from his parents' office.

That office no longer existed. It had come crashing down along with the rest of the Tower of Dedi. Alex's parents had been agents of MAGE—Magic Antiquities Guardianship Enforcement—and not archeologists, as Alex had always been told. They'd hunted down magical artifacts and returned them to the Conjurian, all the while truly searching for the Eye of Dedi.

Well, they'd found it. And hidden it. Hidden it so well that no one had been able to find it since. That was good—at least creepy guys like the Shadow Conjurer had not been able to get their hands on it.

And it was bad, because was Alex really going to be able to find it when no one else ever had?

Yes. Yes, he was, because he had something the Shadow Conjurer didn't, that Christopher Agglar hadn't: clues that his parents had left for him.

Once he got to Plomboria, he'd find those clues. In the meantime, he might as well read, since it didn't seem as if he was going to get any more rest.

Yawning, he opened the book that had been in his pocket, its pages warped and still damp from their dunking in the river. On the cover was the title: *Practical Magic Methods: How Not to Get Burned at the Stake* by Jermay Lucas.

Alex flipped through the book, settled on "Bobo's Coin Switch," then studied the instructions five times. He found a penny and a nickel in his pocket and began to practice while Neil snored and Pimawa twitched and mumbled in his sleep and Emma, curled in a ball with her back to Alex, didn't stir.

After twenty minutes Alex felt like he was getting the knack of the trick. Beside him, Pimawa stretched and yawned under a fraying blanket. He opened one eye and watched Alex for a moment.

"It would seem you have a natural ability for coin sleight," he said.

"Yeah, well," said Alex, "it's just a dumb trick. Like that

stuff that magician does, the one Emma loves so much—
Angel Xavier. Stage magic. It's not going to solve anything."

"Oh no, you are mistaken." Pimawa sat up and straightened his jacket. "Angel Xavier is a true magician. One of the
few whose powers remain. That is probably why the Shadow
Conjurer abducted him."

Alex blinked. "Really?" He thought back to all the TV
shows Emma used to make him watch, with Angel levitating
beautiful assistants or escaping from chains. "He's from here?
The Conjurian? And he got kidnapped? When? Emma and
I were just watching him on TV at Uncle Mordo's. Right
before we. Um. Left."

"Yes, certainly. He vanished, presumed abducted, very
shortly after the three of us, um, arrived," Pimawa answered
somberly. "I am not surprised you missed the news—you
had quite a lot on your mind at the time. As for those tricks—
how 'dumb' they are is a matter of perspective. They have
saved many magicians from the executioner or the stake.
Every magician in the Conjurian learns sleight of hand if he
or she ventures into the Flatworld. Being able to explain away
their powers as simple tricks or illusions has saved many
lives."

Alex picked up the penny with his right hand and dropped
it into his left, where it changed into the nickel. "And people
always bought these explanations? Nobody ever suspected?"

"Certainly. Any explanation, no matter how absurd, is
easier for most Flatworlders to accept than a belief in magic.
You yourself were quite convinced that a Myst fish was a

41

delusion born of moldy bread, even when you were riding one."

Alex nodded. "Okay. The fish was real. But I had a right to be skeptical, didn't I? Look at that mentalist, Tenyo." He had to hold back a shiver as he remembered the girl, not much older than Emma, her face entirely covered by a black veil. Her act had been spooky and unnerving, but it hadn't been real. "She was supposed to read my mind, but she couldn't do a thing except use tricks like these." He slapped the book. "She had everybody fooled. Except me."

Pimawa nodded soberly. "True. So many magicians have had their powers fade to nothing in the last few years. She was one of many."

"And nobody knows why?"

Pimawa shook his head. "Nobody."

"Huh." Alex flipped his coins from hand to hand. "So do you think . . . that could be why the Shadow Conjurer is doing all this?"

Pimawa cocked his head. "I do not quite understand."

Alex frowned, letting the idea take shape in his mind. "Well, the Eye is supposed to bring back magic, right? That's what people think."

"Some people, yes," Pimawa agreed.

"That's what my mom and dad thought."

"I believe so."

"Maybe the Shadow Conjurer thinks so too. Maybe he wants to be the one who brings magic back. Maybe he even thinks that if he can get the Eye, then magicians will be the

powerful ones. They won't have
to hide their powers at all."

"That is . . . a very interesting
theory, Master Alex," Pimawa said.

"Interesting indeed," a new voice
chimed in.

Derren had been stretched out on the floor
next to Savachia. Apparently he'd been listening
to the whole conversation, because he sat up now
and studied Alex with a thoughtful look on his
face.

Before Alex could ask Derren what was up,
the hatch in the ceiling opened, scattering the
shadows. Neil poked his head in, his few greasy
hairs dangling like baby snakes. "Morning! Next
stop, Plomboria!"

The last sleepers woke. Emma and Alex
headed for the ladder.

"Aren't you coming, Pim?" asked Emma, pausing with a
foot on the ladder.

"Yes." Pimawa rose, leaving the blanket draped over his
shoulders. "Of course."

CHAPTER 4

EMMA

Emma balanced on the gently rocking deck as Gertie drew them toward an island looming on the horizon. Soon the alpaca was paddling through a narrow channel between two towering cliffs that led into a bay encircled by waterfalls. Two rock columns rose from the center of the bay. Large circular platforms connected

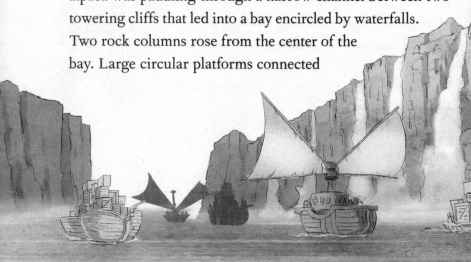

by webs of rope bridges and hundreds of wooden decks mush-roomed out from the columns.

Emma knew that the Shadow Conjurer was probably chasing them. That they'd left much of Conjurian City in ruins behind them. But even so, she couldn't help the smile spreading across her face.

This place was amazing.

A fishing boat, nets hanging from long, drooping poles, rowed past. The Jimjarian crew waved. Emma waved back.

"This is stunning," she said, rubbing her arms in the chilly morning air. "I've never seen anything like it."

"Indeed," said Pimawa, draping his blanket over Emma's shoulders. "I had almost forgotten."

"When was the last time you came home?" asked Emma, turning her head to look up at Pimawa.

"Not since I left with Master Mordo." Pimawa wiped the damp from his eyes. "I wasn't able to return, not even when my mother was ill. I missed her funeral too."

"I'm sorry." Emma placed her hand on Pimawa's paw. "I didn't know."

She felt a rush of shame. Ever since she and Alex had arrived in the Conjurian, Pimawa had been looking out for them. And she'd never even thought to ask about his family or his life before he'd started working for Uncle Mordo.

Alex had told her, last night, that Pimawa's father was none too pleased with his son. He thought that Pimawa wasn't traditional enough. That he hadn't been devoted enough to serving the magician who was his master.

It was ridiculous. Emma had never known anyone as devoted and loyal as Pimawa. And his father's attitude made it even sadder that Pimawa's mother was gone.

Emma knew what it was like to miss a mother.

"It was ... bearable," said Pimawa, his eyes on the waterfalls. "My duty was to keep watch over both of you. She understood."

"Pim, are you okay?" asked Emma.

Pimawa's head and ears drooped. "I never imagined coming home like this. I never thought my father might not want me to come home."

Emma wished she had some comfort to offer. All she could think to do was pat Pimawa's hand as the carriage joined the line of boats heading toward the docks.

Most were flat barges piled high with plants and flowers. Others were stacked precariously with crates. The rising sun mixed with the mist coming off the waterfalls, giving the city a sparkling sheen.

Alex broke the silence, counting the boats streaming into the harbor. "Wow, do they have to import everything?"

"Most of that is for the Choosing ceremony," said Pimawa.

"The what?" asked Alex.

"Remember, Alex?" Emma asked. "Pimawa told us about it before. When a Jimjarian is chosen to serve a magician. Is it happening soon, Pim?"

"Oh my," said Pimawa. "I had lost track of time. Yes, it must be in the next few days."

"They'll have a ceremony now?" Alex asked. "I mean ...

the Shadow Conjurer just took over Conjurian City. And the Tower fell. And everything. But they don't know that yet, do they?"

"It would appear not," Pimawa said, scanning the harbor. "I imagine we are first with the news. Most boats could not make the crossing to Plomboria as quickly as this mechanism did."

"Will they go on with the ceremony once they hear what happened?" Emma asked.

"Miss Emma, of course they will. Nothing in a Jimjarian's life can equal the importance of the Choosing ceremony. It would not be canceled unless Plomboria suddenly sank into the sea."

All three of them remained silent as Neil climbed up on deck to settle himself in the driver's seat and navigate the busy waters. By the time Gertie had pulled the carriage alongside

an open dock, a crowd had gathered to greet them.

Someone yelled, "Is that Pimawa Fornesworth?" Jimjarians crowded onto the dock, helping to tie Gertie up to a piling. Three familiar faces pushed to the front.

Emma had last seen them in Conjurian City, just before Savachia kidnapped her.

"Hello again!" said the wide-eyed Jimjarian. "Oh, we are so thrilled to see you! I'm Rofflo."

"Yes, hello! I am Jukstra," said the creature beside him. "We weren't properly introduced before."

"And I am Royan, at your service," said the third with a slight bow. "We felt horrible after what happened."

"After you"—Jukstra pointed at Emma—"got kidnapped, we took Master Fornesworth's advice and headed straight back here. We've been practicing for our Choosing nonstop."

"Except when we've been working, of course." Royan tipped his orange cap. "We're dockhands, and it's been exceedingly busy."

"Yes, so anything you need," said Jukstra, bowing slightly, "anything at all, just ask."

Derren and Rowlfin emerged from the carriage, followed by Clive. Savachia came next. Several furry hands helped Emma and Alex leap from the carriage to the dock.

Most of the Jimjarians seemed fascinated by Pimawa. They scrambled to shake his hand and pat him on the back. Several little Jimjarians peeked out from behind legs, staring in wonder at him.

"You're like a rock star," said Emma.

Pimawa winced. "Of sorts, yes. It is only because I was chosen by your uncle. He was, at the time, the most famous magician in both worlds."

"Sure, okay," Alex said. He lowered his voice. "But the Shadow Conjurer is probably still on our tail, so when you're done signing autographs, maybe we can do what we came here to do."

"Alex," Emma hissed. Her little brother could be so insensitive. "Pim hasn't been home in a long time. Maybe he should enjoy it a little."

"Honestly, Miss Emma," said Pimawa, "Master Alex is correct. Given all that has transpired, we do not have time to waste."

But Emma knew that this was not how Pimawa had pictured his return. "Don't you want to go home? Before we start hunting for Alex's clues? He doesn't even know where to start, anyway."

"Not particularly." Pimawa glanced over at his father, who was talking to a very official-looking Jimjarian.

As his chat ended, Rowlfin turned toward them. "You." He pointed at his son. "Keep these two in sight. Bring them to the house. Master Fallow and I are going to meet the elder." He nodded at Derren, who gestured for Rowlfin to lead the way, and the two of them set off through the crowd. Emma, Alex, Pimawa, the Grubians, and Savachia stood looking after them.

"Derren wants us to sit around your house?" Alex was frowning. "I don't think so. We have to search for clues right away."

"Really, Alex?" Emma looked at her brother impatiently. "So where do you propose we start?"

She saw with satisfaction that her brother couldn't answer her question. They'd come to Plomboria because Alex had said so, but he didn't have any idea what to do next.

"We could go with Derren and Pimawa's dad," Emma suggested. Alex would see that she could have ideas too. "Who's this elder that they're going to see?"

Pimawa pulled Emma and Alex out of the path of a large wagon loaded with potted plants. "Madame Flarraj. She is our leader."

"Like a president?" asked Alex.

"More like someone we look to for guidance. And, more important, she is in charge of making sure young Jimjarians are prepared to serve magicians."

"What do Derren and Rowlfin want with her?" asked Emma.

"Don't know," said Pimawa. "However, it might be a good idea to get off these docks before we get knocked into the water. We can discuss this more at my home—I mean, my father's house."

"I'm not going to hang around some house, waiting for the Shadow Conjurer to track us down!" Alex announced.

"Well, what *are* you going to do?" Emma challenged him.

"Enough bickering!" Pimawa snapped.

Emma and Alex froze. Heads turned. Emma saw Savachia wipe a quick smirk off his face.

"I do apologize." Pimawa took a deep breath. "Master Alex, Miss Emma, there's someone you should both meet. I wasn't planning on mentioning her, but now I think it might be best. After that, you are free to argue all you want. Is it a deal?"

"Who?" asked Alex.

A smile returned to Pimawa's face. "You'll see. Along the way I'll give you the abbreviated tour." With a fresh spring in his step, Pimawa led the children down a busy street.

The Grubians stayed behind with Gertie and the carriage. Emma turned her head to look back for Savachia. He gave her a jaunty wave before slipping away into the sea of people. Where was he going?

"Don't worry about him," Alex said, when he saw where Emma was staring. "That guy can watch out for himself."

Emma looked all around, gazing at docks that rose several stories on either side. Cranes hung over the edges of the upper stories, hauling cargo from the boats below. They moved onto a large square platform that held a market, where vendors sold all sorts of fish and all the imports brought in by the boats.

Several of the vendors called Pimawa's name as he passed by. Some handed him strange fruits or warm pastries or bunches of flowers. He handed a few of his gifts to the children.

"What is this?" asked Alex, biting into what looked like a wedge of cheese. It was sweet, unlike any kind of cheese Alex had ever had.

"I'll tell you later," said Pimawa with a wink at Emma.

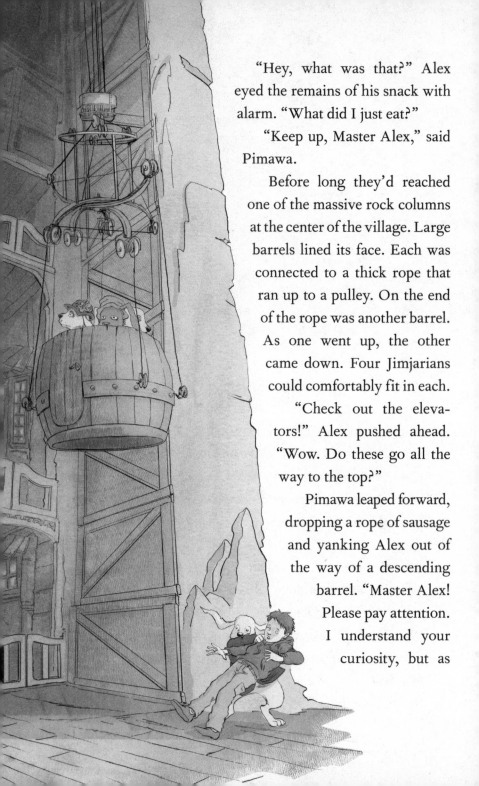

"Hey, what was that?" Alex eyed the remains of his snack with alarm. "What did I just eat?"

"Keep up, Master Alex," said Pimawa.

Before long they'd reached one of the massive rock columns at the center of the village. Large barrels lined its face. Each was connected to a thick rope that ran up to a pulley. On the end of the rope was another barrel. As one went up, the other came down. Four Jimjarians could comfortably fit in each.

"Check out the elevators!" Alex pushed ahead. "Wow. Do these go all the way to the top?"

Pimawa leaped forward, dropping a rope of sausage and yanking Alex out of the way of a descending barrel. "Master Alex! Please pay attention. I understand your curiosity, but as you'll soon see, you need all your wits about you here. Come."

"Seriously?" asked Emma, looking a bit pale. "How high do they go?"

"These only go up four levels," said Pimawa. "The express barrels on the other side of town do go all the way to the top."

Emma shivered. Not long before, she (along with Savachia) had had to climb a rickety catwalk up to the roof of what had once been the grandest theater in Conjurian City, with the Tower guards right behind her. Since then, she felt as if she'd be happy to keep both feet firmly on the ground for the rest of her life.

When he caught sight of the worried expression on Emma's face, Pimawa squeezed her arm. "No worries. With all the platforms, you won't be able to tell how high up you are."

That did not actually make Emma feel much better, but when Pimawa opened the side of a barrel and ushered them inside, she followed him.

Alex reached for a lever. Pimawa knocked his hand away. "Careful, Master Alex. These older lifts don't have all the safety features of the newer ones. Pull that lever too far and we go flying up at full speed."

Alex looked grumpy. "I know how an elevator works."

"Alex, just listen to him," Emma begged. Pimawa eased the lever back, which released the rope brake. The barrel jerked upward.

CHAPTER 5

EMMA

The barrel, with Emma, Alex, and Pimawa inside it, soared skyward, jolting to a stop at an enormous deck packed with Jimjarians.

"Excuse us, please." Pimawa nudged a path through the crowd. The two human children and one Jimjarian wiggled their way around the central column, then climbed a winding stairway carved into the rock. Emma found she was feeling more and more queasy the higher they went. The stone steps were firm beneath her feet, but somehow she expected them to tremble like that fragile metal catwalk in the theater.

She'd arrived in the magical world she'd always dreamed of, just like the heroes in the books she loved, only to discover that she was terrified of heights. Not very heroic. She sighed.

Three more elevator rides brought them to the top of the city, hundreds of feet above the bay. They made their way along the main thoroughfare. Everywhere, Jimjarians were busy decorating for the upcoming ceremony. Garlands of flowers draped decks and ladders; bright banners hung from platforms, rippling in the wind.

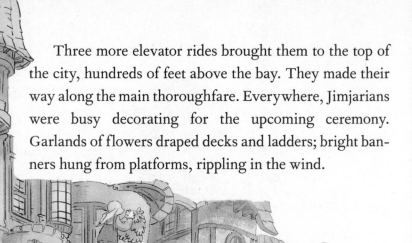

"This way." Pimawa beckoned to them with the arm that wasn't holding all the goods he'd been handed in the marketplace. He stood under an arched opening to a wooden bridge that connected the two rock columns.

Emma gulped. "We have to cross over that?"

"Seriously, Em," said Alex. "We're being hunted by a madman and his crazy flying skeletons and you're worried about a little bridge?"

Emma swatted at her brother's head as he darted past,

following Pimawa onto the narrow, swaying bridge. Emma stood at the edge and took in a shivering breath.

Maybe her parents had been right to send the letter to Alex instead of her. To tell him to take care of her, as if she were a baby. Maybe she wasn't strong enough to handle things here.

But at least she'd try.

Emma stepped onto the crowded bridge. She kept her focus on the far side, where a fan-shaped platform jutted out farther than the rest, covered by an enormous red-and-green awning, like a ship's sail full of wind. Halfway across the bridge, Emma could make out a small army of Jimjarians setting up chairs on that platform, hanging plants in baskets, unrolling banners, and moving crates across the deck.

"What is that?" asked Emma.

"That is where the Choosing ceremony takes place," said Pimawa over his shoulder. "You should see it when it's finished. One of the most glorious sights in Plomboria."

That was when the wooziness hit Emma. At first she thought it was the swaying bridge, the wind gusts, and the sound of crashing waves far below making her head swim.

But soon she knew what it really
was: a feeling of utter and complete sadness.

All these people, these Jimjarians preparing for the big-
gest day of the year, had no idea what was coming. The
Shadow Conjurer, who had destroyed the Tower of Dedi . . .
who had killed Uncle Mordo and Christopher Agglar and
who knew how many others . . . who was still hunting for the
Eye of Dedi to make himself even more powerful . . . that man
was coming here next.

Without a doubt.

He wanted her. He wanted Alex. He wanted them because
he thought they could lead him to the Eye of Dedi. And he'd
do anything to get to them.

Every Jimjarian on Plomboria was at risk, from Pimawa
and Rowlfin to Jukstra and Rofflo and Royan. They were in
danger because Emma and Alex were here.

And what could Emma do about it? What could she do to
stop the Shadow Conjurer?

Nothing.

Not a thing.

Emma clung to the railing of the rope bridge, seeing in
her mind's eye the two stone columns crumbling into the sea.
They would share the same fate as the Tower of Dedi. She

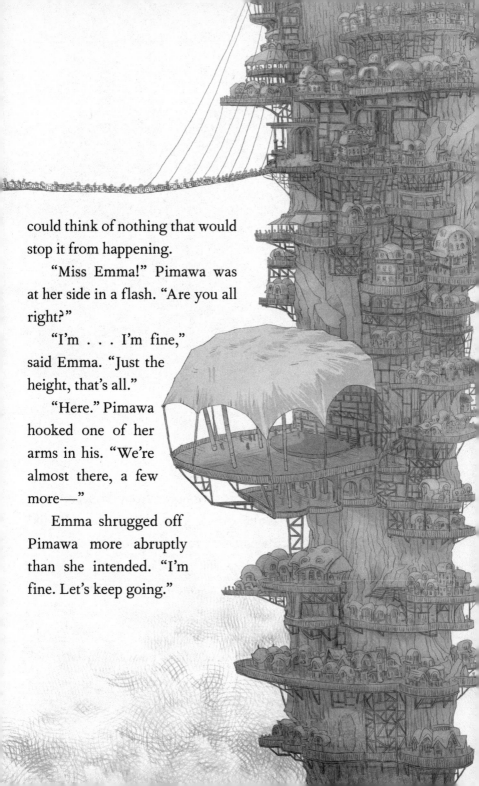

could think of nothing that would
stop it from happening.

"Miss Emma!" Pimawa was
at her side in a flash. "Are you all
right?"

"I'm . . . I'm fine,"
said Emma. "Just the
height, that's all."

"Here." Pimawa
hooked one of her
arms in his. "We're
almost there, a few
more—"

Emma shrugged off
Pimawa more abruptly
than she intended. "I'm
fine. Let's keep going."

ALEX

The decks and platforms that sprang out from the second column were lined with small buildings that looked to Alex like houses. Some had little patches of garden in front.

The crowds thinned as they walked, and soon they arrived at a home encircled by a vine-covered fence. Pimawa unlatched the gate, took four steps to the oval door, and knocked. He smiled at Alex and Emma, waving them close.

Labored shuffling approached from inside. The latch jostled. The door inched open. A gray nose sniffed through the opening. The door creaked inward.

A Jimjarian hobbled over the mossy threshold. Her shoulders were hunched and her eyes were a filmy white. Her fur was thin, revealing wrinkles when she smiled. Her ears hung down on either side of her face.

Alex liked her instantly. He liked her knitted shawl, her green dress, and even her knotted cane.

"Is that . . . ?" She sniffed. "Pimawa! My, what an honor."

"A good day to you, Miss Harrafia. I have brought two guests for you." Pimawa bowed his head, nudging the kids closer to Miss Harrafia.

Miss Harrafia reached out a paw and brushed Emma's face. Alex saw his sister flinch. He was about to hiss at her to stand still when he saw that she'd figured it out. The old Jimjarian was blind.

Miss Harrafia caressed Emma's face, then Alex's. Tears welled on her sagging eyelids.

"Uh, Miss Harrafia?" Emma asked. "Are you okay?"

"Yes, yes. Sorry. Forgive an old woman." Miss Harrafia hobbled aside. "Please come in."

A simple table occupied most of the front room. Dried plants hung over the fireplace. Soft flames tickled the bottom of a copper cauldron.

Miss Harrafia seemed to know exactly where everything in the room was, even though she couldn't see any of it. She slid two stools from under the sink. "Please, sit. Had I known you were arriving today, I would have prepared something." She whacked the cauldron with her cane. "This gruel is not suitable for proper company. Helps with the rust on the joints, though. I am a horrible hostess."

"It's quite all right, Miss Harrafia," said Pimawa, plunking what remained of his perishable gifts on the table. "We brought something to eat."

They made themselves comfortable around the table. Miss Harrafia filled glasses from a stone pitcher. The liquid tasted of flowers and honey, soothing Alex's dry throat. Between them, Alex and Pimawa put a dent in the pile of pastries and cakes.

"I don't suppose you know who I am," said Miss Harrafia, leaning forward.

But Alex had an idea already. "You knew our parents," he said quickly.

Emma sat up straighter and glanced at Pimawa.

He nodded.

"Perceptive boy," she said, wiping some spilled drink

from her shawl. "I was their Jimjarian. My memory falters often these days, but I shall never forget the day of my Choosing. The falls filled the sky with rainbows. So much hope back then.

"My parents had prayed I would end up with the likes of Thurston or Kellar. That turned out to be far from reality, as I failed, ceremony after ceremony. Alas, it seemed that a life of serving a great magician was not for me.

"I remained busy, helping organize and prepare young Jimjarians for their ceremonies for many years. That was until a young couple, attending their first ceremony, spotted me and made a shocking request: to have me as their Jimjarian. Madame Flarraj did not know what to say, other than to agree. I thank Dedi for that day."

She sat silent for a minute, smiling at the memories still in her head. Emma sipped her flower water, looking down at the table. Alex thought she might be fighting back tears.

But they did not have time for tears or sentimental memories. Alex leaned forward. "Excuse me, Miss Harrafia. But did our parents leave information for us about the Eye of Dedi? Like a map, or some kind of clue?"

"I'm sorry, young one, but they did not," said Miss Harrafia, shaking her head.

Alex leaned across the table, rattling the pitcher, trying to ignore Emma's *I told you so* look. "But there must be something. Maybe something you've forgotten . . . ?"

Emma swatted her brother's arm. "Alex, don't be rude!"

"What Master Alex is trying to say," said Pimawa, "is

that we believe Master Henry and Mistress Evelynne may have secreted clues as to the Eye's whereabouts. Did they leave nothing at all behind? It might be something that appears quite unimportant. Miss Harrafia, please, can you think of anything?"

Miss Harrafia remained motionless. Her milky eyes didn't blink. Emma reached for Miss Harrafia's arm.

"You upset her," she whispered fiercely, glaring at Alex.

"All I did was ask a question!" he hissed back.

"Ah!" cried Miss Harrafia, startling Emma off her stool. She stood, withdrawing a key from her shawl, and waddled into a back room.

Alex gave Emma a triumphant look. He perched on the edge of his seat, waiting for her return.

What would she bring? Another letter? A map? A set of instructions? He'd been right to come to Plomboria. In a minute Alex would know his next step.

Miss Harrafia reemerged with a folded blanket, cradling it as if it were a child. She unfolded it on the table.

"They left these," she said with a raspy chuckle. "Yes indeed. I had almost forgotten. Forgive my addled old brain. You see, Master Henry and Miss Evelynne did not tell me the true nature of their work. They told me, as they told the world, that they were simple magicians traveling the world to entertain the masses. But I knew. I knew all along that they had a greater purpose. In truth, they were hunting down magical artifacts that had gone missing in the Flatworld, trying to keep them out of the wrong hands. Artifacts like these. Master Alex, this is for you."

Alex reached out to pick up the object that Miss Harrafia indicated—an old Swiss Army knife.

"And, Miss Emma, this is yours."

Emma gripped the other, a pick small enough to be swung by hand. It looked like something a mountaineer might use.

A pick and a pocketknife? This was not what Alex had been expecting. He'd been hoping for another letter or a map or a list of instructions explaining just where the Eye had been hidden.

Instead he'd gotten a rusty, ancient knife that probably couldn't even cut butter anymore. Emma didn't seem any more thrilled with her inheritance than Alex was. She looked at the pick with distaste.

Miss Harrafia, of course, couldn't see the expressions on their faces. She went on speaking.

"Now I know what Master Henry and Mistress Evelynne's purpose was," she said. She seemed to be looking into the past

with her blind eyes. "To find the Eye of Dedi. To restore the magic that has been fading from the Conjurian all these years. Fading, fading . . ."

Emma dropped the pick on the table with a clang. The noise seemed to startle Miss Harrafia back to the present moment.

"Oh my." Miss Harrafia straightened her shawl. "When Master Henry and Mistress Evelynne went on their last mission to the Flatworld, they told me not to accompany them. Instead I was to take you, Master Alex—wrapped in this very blanket—and your sister to your uncle's house. You didn't make a sound. Your sister wailed. Although, in retrospect, Master Mordo did have that effect on children.

"Master Henry also insisted I take these two items for safekeeping," Miss Harrafia went on. "So that is what I did. I left you with Mordo the Mystifier and returned to the Conjurian to await the arrival of my master and mistress. But they did not come back. They never came back."

Silence wrapped itself around Miss Harrafia's next words, until Pimawa broke it.

"Miss Harrafia," he said softly. "Master Mordo is dead."

Miss Harrafia nodded.

"How did you know?" asked Alex.

"He's not with you." Miss Harrafia folded the blanket. "Master Mordo would never have let these two children out of his sight, much less sent them off into the Conjurian without him. Master Alex, Miss Emma, your safety was his deepest concern. And that of your parents as well. They loved you more than anything in either world. Everything they did, it was for you. To keep you safe."

"They failed," said Emma harshly.

Everyone around the little table jumped. Alex turned to stare at his sister. What was up with her?

"We're not safe here," said Emma. She glared at Miss Harrafia, at Alex, at Pimawa. "We're not safe anywhere. Thanks to them."

Miss Harrafia placed her hand gently on Emma's. "Your parents tried. At least they tried. What else could they do?"

"They could've been parents," said Emma, wrenching her hand away. "They could've forgotten all about this stupid world and stayed with us." Emma flung the blanket on the floor and headed for the door.

Alex knew he should probably go after his sister, but his eyes were riveted on something she had not noticed. Something that had been lying under the blanket all this time.

"Oh dear," Miss Harrafia said. "That poor young thing. Perhaps—"

"Miss Harrafia," Alex interrupted eagerly. "What's this book?"

"Oh," Miss Harrafia said. "That was the only other thing I have from my time with your parents. Reading it used to bring me some comfort before my eyes became too weak to see the words. I thought perhaps you might like to have it."

CHAPTER 6

EMMA

Emma slumped down against the fence.

Long ago, Uncle Mordo had told her that her parents had died. Once Alex had grown up a bit, he'd echoed the same words. They were not coming home. They were dead.

Emma had ignored it all. She'd trusted that they were coming home. With her suitcase ready, packed under her bed, she'd waited and waited and waited.

For nothing. For a grubby old pick and a note addressed to her brother.

Pimawa came through the gate and hunched down next to her. "Miss Emma, are you indisposed?"

She ignored him, instead watching Jimjarians pushing carts full of decorations down the street.

"We should meet up with the others at my house," suggested Pimawa. "We can rest there for a bit."

Emma nodded. What else was there to do?

Alex came out of the house, clutching his stupid jackknife and something else. A slim, leather-bound book that he tried to wave in her face.

"Emma!" he whooped at her. "It's Dad's journal! Em, look!"

Emma turned away. She trudged behind Alex and Pimawa along several winding streets swamped with cheerful Jimjarians heading home for lunch after a long morning of preparing for the ceremony.

The truth was, she didn't want to see some old journal. If she couldn't have the parents who'd lived in her imagination all those years, the ones who were going to swoop in the door at any moment, wrap her up in their arms, and wash away years of loneliness and grief and confusion, then she didn't really want any.

Certainly not ones who'd gone chasing the Eye of Dedi instead of looking after their children. And now Alex wanted to do the very same thing! And he kept waving that journal in her face as if he expected her to be as excited about it as he was. Emma wanted to slug him.

"My home is down the next left." Pimawa slowed his pace.

"Sounds like a party," said Alex, listening to the joyous cries coming from around the bend.

The noise came from a bunch of young Jimjarians clustered around the Grubian brothers as they animated two puppets over their heads. Neil's puppet, a hairy creature with giant fangs, lunged at the kids, who yelped and covered their

long ears. Clive swooped in with the hero, a Jimjarian clad in armor wielding a stubby sword.

"Well, hello!" Neil grinned over his audience at Alex and Emma. Even while his attention was diverted, his puppet kept darting at the audience while avoiding the slashing of Clive's. "Any great revelations as to the whereabouts of the Eye?"

"No," Emma snapped.

"Maybe," Alex countered, holding the journal close.

"Master Grubian, would you kindly keep your voice down?" Pimawa asked. "There is no need to broadcast what we are trying to do. If word got back to"—his voice dropped—"the Shadow Conjurer . . ."

Neil handed his fanged monster over to Clive, who kept the battle raging without missing a beat. The taller Grubian spun away, pulled by the warring puppets. The kids whooped and chased after him.

"I expect such word will reach him very shortly," Neil said, eyeing Pimawa. "Our arrival here was by no means clandestine. It will not take long for an interested party or two to make their way back to Conjurian City with the news of a Jimjarian and two young Flatworlders."

"No Jimjarian on this island would endanger these children!" Pimawa snapped.

Neil shrugged. "Not a one? Not a single one? You have absolute faith in every single one of your long-eared friends? Well, I envy you. But I don't share your trust. Whatever clues you hope to uncover, young Alex, I suggest you do so soon." The short, round man skipped away. "If you need a distraction, come find us," he called over his shoulder.

"That's about all I think we can count on them for," said Emma. "Distraction."

"If there were profit to be made from saving the world," said Alex, "they would lead the charge."

"Shall we?" Pimawa opened the gate to his front yard, which was overwhelmed by shrubs.

"You go on in, Em." Alex sat down on the stairs of the front porch. "I want some quiet to check this out." He patted the journal and pulled the jackknife from his pocket. He snapped open a blade and jabbed it into the steps.

"Fine." Emma stomped up the steps, letting out her frustration in noise.

Then Alex yelped.

"What? Did you cut yourself?" Emma asked without looking back.

"Look!" shouted Alex. She turned. He thrust the knife at her. Emma's heart skipped a beat and she jumped back. "Watch it, stupid!"

"Calm down, Master Alex!" said Pimawa.

"No way! I'm not calming down!" Alex held the knife at eye level, running his finger along one of the blades. "There's something written here. Numbers. Coordinates!"

Emma snatched at the knife, feeling jealousy squirm in her stomach. All the clues—letter, journal, now knife—were for her brother! She could barely make out the tiny numbers carved into the metal, but if she squinted she could see an *N* and a *17*, and then an *E* and a *7*. "How

N,17,E,7

74

do you know these are coordinates?" she asked skeptically. "They could be anything."

Alex's eyebrows dipped as he tilted his head. "Seriously? You don't think I know what map coordinates look like?" His excitement resumed. "Pim, Jimjarians must have lots of maps. I mean, you live on an island. You've got to have charts of the sea around here, right?"

"Well, yes." Pimawa hesitated. "There are the archives. I would suppose that—"

"Great! Let's go!" Alex jumped up, ready to head back toward the street.

"Hang on," called Emma. "You really think Mom and Dad hid the location of the Eye of Dedi on a pocketknife?"

Alex grinned. "Yeah, I do. I *know* Mom and Dad left that note, *knowing* I would find their office and go poking around. They sent us here *knowing* we'd meet Miss Harrafia and get the knife. So yes, I *know* that Mom and Dad told us where to go next."

"Great," Emma snapped. "I'm thrilled that *you're* part of Mom and Dad's master plan." She swatted the pick dangling from her belt. "I suppose they left me this so I could hang around here and play in a sandbox or something!"

She hated the look of pity that swept over Alex's face.

Her brother sighed. "Emma, come on. Okay, I get how you're feeling. But we don't have time for this. We have a clue! What matters is we have a chance, a real chance to get the Eye. Pimawa, can you take me to the archives?"

Pimawa looked anxiously from Alex to Emma. "Miss Emma. It does seem worth checking. Won't you—"

"I'm not going to some old archive," Emma said sulkily. She knew she was behaving like a brat, and she didn't really care.

"But I must look after both of you. I must keep you safe."

Emma sighed. "I'll stay here, okay? Derren and your dad should be here anytime."

"Very well. Please, Miss Emma, do not go anywhere. Wait for us. We won't be long." Alex had already taken off, headed back up the street. Pimawa bounded after him. "Master Alex, you're going the wrong way!"

ALEX

The archives were a couple of levels below where Pimawa lived. This was an older section of the city, the building rougher and plainer than the ones above—at least until they got to an ornately carved door that led directly into the tall rock column.

On the other side of the door, an oblong room had been hollowed out of the bluish-gray stone. A small kiosk stood in the middle, with a stout Jimjarian behind it, giving them a startled look over silver-rimmed glasses.

"Are you two lost?" asked the clerk.

Pimawa hesitated. "Ah, no. That is . . . we were hoping to investigate something in the archives."

"The archives are only open by appointment," the Jimjarian said shortly.

Alex paused for a moment. This was the first grumpy Jimjarian he had encountered. Well, the second if you included Pimawa's dad. He'd gotten so used to how helpful Jimjarians tended to be that it was a bit of a shock to meet one who didn't intend to do what Alex wanted.

Then Alex remembered how he and Pimawa had gotten out of the Tower. Every Tower guard had been hunting for Alex, ready to lock him back up—but Pimawa had told him what to do. And it had worked.

Alex assumed that the same advice would work here. *Belief can define truth*. And he truly believed he needed to get into the archives.

Alex squared his shoulders and continued walking right past the clerk. "Of course we know that. But we were sent by Mordo the Mystifier to do some critical research. There was no time for an appointment. Lives are at stake." Alex tried to sound annoyed.

The guard stepped out from behind the desk, blocking the door behind him. "I'm afraid I'll need to see—" Suddenly he stopped talking and beamed at Pimawa. "Oh, I didn't recognize you at first! Will Mordo the Mystifier be joining you?"

Pimawa tugged the clerk's sleeve, making him lean close. "Unfortunately not. This is very delicate research for the Circle, and it's critical no one know about it. Especially that Master Mordo is involved. The fate of the Conjurian may be at stake."

The ploy worked. The guard straightened. "You can count on me. I won't tell a soul you were here." He rattled the key ring from his belt, then fumbled the correct key into a lock in the wall behind the kiosk.

"Thank you," said Pimawa. "We will tell Master Mordo how helpful you were."

The clerk was still beaming when he closed the door behind them. The walls were cold and damp, the passage lit by diamond-shaped lanterns.

"That was good thinking," said Alex. "The fewer people who know we're in here, the better."

"Do you think the Shadow Conjurer could actually have spies in Plomboria?" Pimawa asked, frowning.

"He found us at Uncle Mordo's," said Alex. "He knew I was in the Tower. I assume he had help getting that info."

They climbed down the steps spiraling along the wall. The air grew colder as they went, and smelled of moss. Armor-clad Jimjarians had been carved into the rock.

Eventually the stairs ended. The rock floor was smooth. The air was unnervingly still. Alex and Pimawa passed into a vast cavern, full of shelves that followed a spiral path. Each shelf was lined with square compartments, and each compartment was labeled with a number and stuffed with slender copper tubes.

"How are these organized?" he asked.

"Sorry, Master Alex," Pimawa answered. "I don't know."

Alex strode along the shelves, checking each label, until they reached the center. A sculpture made up of seven standing stones filled most of the space. The stones were about knee-height to Alex, and their tops had been carved into

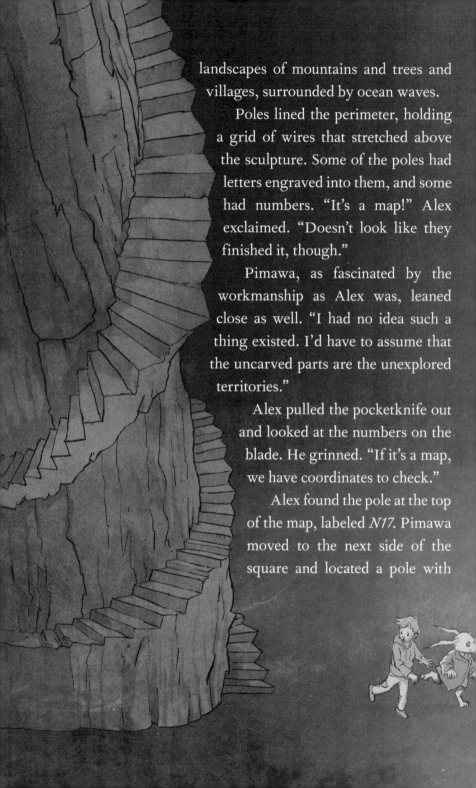

landscapes of mountains and trees and villages, surrounded by ocean waves.

Poles lined the perimeter, holding a grid of wires that stretched above the sculpture. Some of the poles had letters engraved into them, and some had numbers. "It's a map!" Alex exclaimed. "Doesn't look like they finished it, though."

Pimawa, as fascinated by the workmanship as Alex was, leaned close as well. "I had no idea such a thing existed. I'd have to assume that the uncarved parts are the unexplored territories."

Alex pulled the pocketknife out and looked at the numbers on the blade. He grinned. "If it's a map, we have coordinates to check."

Alex found the pole at the top of the map, labeled *N17*. Pimawa moved to the next side of the square and located a pole with

E7 engraved on its surface. Alex followed the wire attached to his pole over to where it intersected the wire attached to Pimawa's.

"Here!" Alex turned in a circle. "This is the spot!"

"Are you certain?" said Pimawa, staring at the empty space underneath the intersecting wires. "That's in the unexplored regions! No one has ever come back from there."

"There's a first time for everything." Alex peered at the floor. Another grid, corresponding to the wires overhead, had been gouged into the ground. Each section had a different number carved into it. "Ninety-three! Pimawa, I bet we need shelf ninety-three." Alex backed away from the sculpture and ran to the shelves. "I'm sure our friend upstairs won't mind if we take one of these with us."

Pimawa hurried after him. "What did you mean by 'take one with us'? With us . . . into the unexplored regions? I must remind you, Master Alex, that hunting for clues in archives and libraries differs greatly from actually undertaking such an expedition. People come *back* from the library."

Alex ignored Pimawa, hurrying along the shelves. Something rustled in the dimness. "Did you hear that?" he asked.

Pimawa's long, sensitive ears twitched. "Hear what? No, I didn't," he answered.

Surely a giant rabbit's hearing would be more sensitive than his own, Alex thought. So if Pimawa hadn't heard a thing, there was nothing to hear. Alex returned to his search. He ran his finger along the dusty engraved numbers on the compartments that lined the shelves until he found the right one. He pulled out a long tube with ornate, tarnished end caps. "Here it is! Next stop, the unexplored regions!"

Pimawa took the tube from Alex and slid it back into its slot. "We are not going to the unexplored regions," he said firmly.

Alex pulled the tube back out. "Maybe you're not, but I am."

"Master Alex," said Pimawa, "your parents didn't go through all that trouble to keep you hidden so you could get lost at sea."

Alex almost lost the tug-of-war for the tube. "My parents wanted me to find this chart. They addressed the letter to me. They left the knife for me. You're acting like Emma. We don't have a choice here! We have to go where Mom and Dad are telling us to go!"

Somewhere in the distance, they heard the distinct sound of a copper tube clattering to the stony floor. Dust that had remained undisturbed for who knew how long drifted through the yellow light. Alex stifled a cough.

Something was coming.

CHAPTER 7

EMMA

As soon as Emma pushed open the door to Pimawa's house, she could see that the inside was the complete opposite of the overgrown yard. No matter how busy Pimawa's dad was, he kept his house ready for company.

A fire glowed in the oval fireplace to her right. Across from the entrance was an arched doorway tucked under the stairs. Pictures had been hung along the staircase; Emma went up a few steps to study one where a pretty bunny in a flowered dress held something in a blanket that looked like a cotton ball with eyes. Pimawa as a baby?

The place was silent. Nobody seemed to be at home. Presumably Derren and Rowlfin were still meeting with the elder—what was her name again? Madame Flarraj? Neil and

Clive were out entertaining children with their puppets, Savachia
was doing who knew what, and
Alex and Pimawa were hunting
for clues to the whereabouts of
the Eye of Dedi.

It was only Emma who had
nothing to do.

She sat down on the stairs and
sighed.

Nothing at all.

Weirdly, the only thing that
came to her mind was Angel
Xavier.

She used to love watching
Angel's stage shows as much
as she loved reading fantasy
novels. Well, so had everybody else. Angel was the
most popular magician in
the world—in her old
world. The Flatworld. She
hadn't known then what Alex
had told her—that Angel was
really from here. The Conjurian.

Uncle Mordo had never
wanted his wards to watch TV,
but whenever Alex's contraband
set had been working, Emma

85

would watch breathlessly as Angel turned a glass of spilled milk into fluttering doves or escaped from an underwater tank or made the Eiffel Tower vanish. Because as long as Angel was onstage, magic was real. Death could be dodged. Nothing dreadful or dangerous could actually happen.

Now Emma was in a place where magic actually *was* real. And the show was not entertaining. Angel himself had vanished, according to Alex—taken by the Shadow Conjurer, probably. And the plot didn't seem to be working out. The villain was too scary, the danger was too real, and it looked like her little brother—not Emma herself—was the hero of the story.

Emma wasn't sure how long she'd been sitting on the stairs when the door opened. Rowlfin came in, with Derren behind him. Geller swooped in over Derren's head.

"Emma, good," Derren said. "Where's Alex? And Savachia? Please come inside, Madame Flarraj."

An elderly Jimjarian wearing what must have been the brightest robe in all of Plomboria

followed Derren into the front room. Rowlfin, murmuring something about tea, disappeared through a door opposite the fireplace. Geller perched on the mantel and scratched his beak with a claw.

"I don't know where Savachia went," Emma said listlessly, answering Derren. "Alex and Pimawa are hunting for some old map or something. He thought he found a clue on a pocketknife."

Derren stiffened.

"I told you both to come straight here!" he said angrily. "What's Alex trying to do? Get himself killed? Doesn't he realize how dangerous things are?"

Emma felt like pointing out that things had been dangerous in Conjurian City, too, when Derren had told her he could not help her. Had told her to leave and fend for herself. But she just didn't have the energy to argue.

Derren must have seen something of what she was feeling in her face. Quickly, he came to her side.

"Emma, I know I let you down. I can't ever tell you how sorry I am. I thought it was the right thing to do at the time, but I now know how wrong I was. I'll look after you, I promise I will. You can count on me."

Back in Conjurian City, Emma would have given almost anything to hear those words from Derren. To her surprise, now they didn't make her feel anything at all.

"Emma," Derren pressed on, "where has Alex gone?"

"To the archives," she answered. "Alex and Pimawa went to the archives."

ALEX

Pimawa quietly slid another metal tube from a nearby shelf, gripping it like a club. He stepped in front of Alex. In the distance, they heard more metal tubes crashing and rolling across the rock floor.

"It must be a Rag-O-Roc," whispered Alex.

"Hush," warned Pimawa.

"Why? It knows we're in here."

"I'll hold it off," whispered Pimawa. "You get out. Run as fast as you can. Get your sister and go to my father. He'll be able to get you both out of Plomboria."

Alex nodded, feeling guilty for agreeing so quickly. But Pimawa was right. If the Rag-O-Rocs had found them already, the Shadow Conjurer wasn't far behind. Alex had to get himself and his sister as far away as they could go, as quickly as possible.

Tapping and clicking noises moved closer, winding inward along the spiral.

"Master Alex, right as it comes around the curve, I shall charge," said Pimawa. "While it's distracted, you must flee."

Alex wished Pimawa hadn't used the word *flee*. Not so heroic. Then again, considering the way every muscle in his body was ready to run, he knew he was no hero.

A wispy shadow edged around the curve of the shelves. With a cry that startled Alex, Pimawa lunged forward. Alex, however, did not stir.

He knew that he should be running, darting past Pimawa,

dodging the Rag-O-Roc, and racing along the spiral of shelves. But his brain was flashing images of the way Christopher Agglar had died, with Rag-O-Rocs flocking around him until he'd disappeared beneath their tattered black robes. Freezing terror locked Alex in place. Any chance of escape was gone.

The creature fluttered into view, and Pimawa swung the map container wildly, missing his target and splintering a shelf instead. Piercing squawks erupted as Pimawa turned to make another attack. However, he was face to face not with a Rag-O-Roc but with a terrified parrot, who flew in a sharp loop over his head to avoid the swinging metal canister.

Geller landed hard on the rock map, skidding to a stop on the crystal ocean.

"For the love of Dedi," said Geller, balancing his glasses on his beak, "why is it, boy, that you and your sister *and* your friends seem convinced that I am a mortal enemy? Have none of you ever seen a parrot before?"

"Sorry—oh, I'm sorry!" Pimawa dropped the canister and rushed to the bird's aid. "I am so glad I missed."

"*You're* glad? How do you imagine I feel?" Geller hopped away from Pimawa.

"Why were you spying on us?" Alex picked up the canister that Pimawa had dropped.

"Spying?" Geller squawked. "I was not *spying*. Master Derren sent me to fetch you." Geller shook the dirt from his feathers.

"What does Derren want?" asked Alex.

"He and Rowlfin are meeting with Madame Flarraj to secure a safe place for you and your sister to stay."

"A place to stay?" Alex drew back as if he had smelled four-week-old garbage. "Well, you're going to have to fly back and inform them we have a different plan."

"Master Alex," said Pimawa, "maybe it would be best to hear them out. At the very least, staying in Plomboria might give you more time to find more clues."

Alex paced over to the shelves, found the correct canister, and tucked it under his arm. "Never mind, Geller, I'll inform them myself what the plan is. There aren't any more clues on this island, Pimawa. We don't need any more. I found what I need, and now it's time to go get the Eye."

EMMA

Emma still sat on the stairs of Rowlfin's house, because she didn't feel as if she had the energy to get up and go elsewhere. She was listening to Derren and Rowlfin talk to Madame Flarraj.

"I—I—" Madame Flarraj shook her head. "This is an awful lot to take in. How could the Tower of Dedi be gone? I'm certain Master Agglar would have contacted us. . . ."

"Madame Flarraj." Rowlfin bowed his head. "I'm afraid we lost Master Agglar."

Madame Flarraj looked more confused than ever. "Yes, Master Derren mentioned that, yet I don't see . . . How could the Circle allow . . ."

"Madame Flarraj, please listen. I am all that is left of the Circle. The only one still alive." Derren leaned toward the Jimjarian elder. "And I am asking for your help."

"Oh, of course." Madame Flarraj blinked at him. "Of course. It's just . . . it's a trifle . . . inconvenient." She placed a hand on the wall as if to stabilize herself. "Didn't you see all those boats at the dock? And more arriving? The Choosing ceremony is tomorrow. Yes. The Choosing ceremony. Really, you must all come to the ceremony. You will be honored guests. After that, well, we will see what we can do."

"Listen, please," said Derren in tones of strained patience. "We may not have time to wait for the Choosing ceremony to be over. The Shadow Conjurer is no doubt searching the entire Conjurian for Emma and Alex. We need to make sure they are safely hidden before he comes here."

"The Shadow Conjurer? Here? Surely not. I think you must be mistaken," Madame Flarraj said, blinking her wide eyes. "We are only a small island. Only Jimjarians. What would a magician like the"—her voice dropped to a whisper—"Shadow Conjurer want here?"

"He wants us," Emma said from the staircase. "He wants my brother and me. He thinks we know where the Eye of Dedi is."

Madame Flarraj turned to look at her, startled. "Oh. My. Er . . . do you? Know? Where it is?"

Emma shook her head.

Then the front door banged open, making everyone jump. Alex rushed inside, clutching a long copper tube in one hand. Geller flapped over his head. Pimawa came behind.

"I know where it is!" Alex said, waving his tube. "The Eye!"

"Master Alex, keep your voice down! Please!" Pimawa shut the door.

Derren was on his feet. "You know *what*? And what were you doing in the archives? I told you to come here!"

Alex ignored the question and jabbed his canister at Derren. "This will lead us right to it. I found the coordinates on a knife that Mom and Dad left for me, and then Pimawa and I talked our way into the archives and found the location,

and then we thought a Rag-O-Roc had found us, but it was only Geller. We need a ship and supplies and, oh, a well-seasoned crew would be a plus, and—"

Derren placed his hands on Alex's shoulders. "Take a breath."

Alex looked around with a baffled expression on his face. Emma had seen that look before, when he was trying to tell her about some fascinating new contraption he'd built but all she wanted to do was read.

"We'll go over all this later," said Derren. "Right now we have to make plans to find you and your sister somewhere safe, where the Shadow Conjurer won't find you."

"Yeah, trust me, no one will find us here!" Alex tapped the canister.

Derren turned back to Madame Flarraj. "Please forgive them. They've been through a lot in the past few days." Then he turned to Pimawa. "Take the kids upstairs and let them rest. Do *not* let them out of your sight."

The side of Rowlfin's lip curled. "Yes, for Dedi's sake, Pimawa. You have one job. Go do it!"

"Rowlfin and I will keep talking with Madame Flarraj," Derren went on. "We'll figure out a place for you to stay."

Alex stood still. "Stay? We don't need to stay anywhere. We've got to get moving!"

"Alex. Upstairs. Now."

Alex stared at Derren, his shock slowly changing to outrage. Emma heaved herself up off the steps.

"Come on, Alex. He's not going to help you. Any more than he helped me."

A pained look crossed Derren's face. "Emma, please. I am *trying* to help him. I'm trying to help you both."

"Yeah," Emma said wearily, "I know." She turned her attention to her brother. "Come on, Alex. Listen to him."

"Listen to him? Why should I listen to him?" Alex shifted impatiently. "Emma, I found the next clue!"

Emma shook her head. "Alex, don't you get it? We're just a couple of kids. It's like you keep telling me—this isn't some fantasy novel where everything comes out all right in the end. Or a magic show where the lady gets sawed in half and put together like nothing ever happened. We're not going to fight off the Shadow Conjurer. And we're not going on a quest for the Eye, either. We might as well just go to sleep. There's nothing else to do."

CHAPTER 8

ALEX

"I'm afraid it is not as spacious as Master Mordo's estate," said Pimawa. He pushed Alex's head down, preventing him from banging it on the low beams arching over the stairs. "When I became his assistant I got lost in his house five times in the first week. No chance of that here."

There was no argument from Alex, as he hunched to fit into the hallway on the second floor.

Pimawa opened two adjacent doors. "These will be your rooms. A bit cramped, sorry."

"We won't be here long anyway, so it doesn't really matter," Alex said. He entered the room Pimawa showed him. It was round, with a short bed that faced a circular window covered by a thick purple curtain. A nightstand that looked like a giant spool, empty of thread, filled the space between the door and bed. A pitcher of water and a glass rested on a silver serving cart under the window.

Alex laid the copper tube with the map inside it carefully across the nightstand. Emma went into her own room without saying good night. Or anything at all.

Alex might have been worried about her, if he hadn't been so irritated at her for taking Derren's side. He flopped onto his back on the bed.

"Master Alex," said Pimawa.

Alex picked up his head and looked at the Jimjarian.

"You did very well to find the coordinates and the map," Pimawa said softly. "Do not despair. Tomorrow, just after the Choosing ceremony is over, we will develop a plan of action."

Alex let his head fall back on the mattress. It practically bounced. The bed was as hard as packed dirt.

"Thanks, Pim," he said.

Pimawa nodded and closed the door.

Alex couldn't believe it. He just couldn't. He'd found his parents' note. He'd found the coordinates on the pocketknife. He'd found the map. And now Derren wanted him to hide away like a good little boy, instead of searching for the one thing that could help them all—the Eye of Dedi!

Well, that wasn't going to happen.

Alex tugged his father's journal out of his pocket. If he was going to sleep at all—and he'd better get some rest, or he wouldn't be in any shape to go looking for the Eye—he needed to read a little first. He flipped open the journal.

The last page made Alex's breath stop in his throat.

There, sketched in black ink on white paper, was the Eye of Dedi.

It looked like a rock. That was all. Alex remembered Neil and Clive Grubian's puppet show, which had shown him and Emma how the Eye came to be. It had been nothing more than an ordinary pebble that Dedi had picked up from the floor of his prison cell—until Dedi had packed all his magical abilities inside it, filling it up with the power to create the Conjurian.

In his father's drawing, the Eye looked ordinary, all right—a dull gray pebble with a dark band that ran like a belt all around it. Notes surrounded it.

This was the thing that Alex was looking for. The thing that his parents had died for.

97

And now Alex knew where to go to find it. All he had to do was convince everyone to let him try.

EMMA

The next morning, Emma sat with Pimawa on the high platform she had seen the day before, waiting for the Choosing ceremony to start. A stage had been erected, and Jimjarians darted over and around it. Some were setting up towering floral displays while others carted large trunks of magical apparatuses behind the curtains.

One Jimjarian rolled a huge dolly out onto the stage. A pair of tubes, one red and one yellow, each big enough to hold a person, perched on it. The rabbit parked the dolly next to a table that another Jimjarian had just draped with a black cloth spangled with stars.

Two more Jimjarians came staggering toward the table, each holding one handle of a huge, brightly painted trunk. They heaved the trunk onto the table.

Wind shook the green-and-red striped awning over the stage. From the edge of the awning, metal cables had been strung up to the highest deck the elevator could reach. Bright red paper lanterns swung from these cables, bobbing in the moving air.

It was colorful. It was festive. It was exciting. Emma watched it all without feeling the slightest interest.

Derren was on Pimawa's other side, with Rowlfin next to him. Madame Flarraj sat on the aisle, dressed in a robe even brighter than the one she'd worn yesterday.

Alex was not there. He'd elected to stay in his room at Rowlfin's house, shouting several uncomplimentary things through the door about going to see a silly stage show when they could be looking for the Eye.

Emma sighed and shifted in her seat. She understood why Alex was so upset . . . but was he really imagining that he'd be able to stock a ship and sail off to find the Eye? That Derren would let him do any such thing?

She could hardly believe she was the one telling Alex he

was being ridiculous. Impractical. A dreamer. Usually it was the other way around.

But Emma felt as if she'd grown up several hundred years in the past few days. Maybe she understood some things now that her brother did not.

In the meantime, she was going to sit here and watch a magic show. Because that was what everybody kept telling her to do.

ALEX

Alex lay on his bed, staring at the ridiculously purple drapes. He'd promised to stay at Rowlfin's house until they all returned from the Choosing ceremony. He'd promised not to go looking for the Eye by himself . . . yet. So he was stuck here.

Alex sat up on the edge of the bed and poured himself a glass of water from the pitcher on the nightstand. At least he could do that for himself.

There was one other thing he could do, something he'd once sworn he wouldn't. Before he'd come to the Conjurian, whenever he was frustrated or unhappy or sick of his uncle Mordo's rules, one thing had always made him feel better.

Fixing something.

Alex pulled out his father's pocket watch. It was the one physical connection he had to his parents. A memory frozen in time, literally. He'd always believed that if he repaired the watch, he would somehow lose whatever connection he had to his parents.

But now he had the journal, and the knife, and the map coordinates. He had a new inheritance from his parents—a quest to save the world. The watch wasn't the only thing they'd left him. And if he got it fixed, he could use it when he went off to find the Eye.

Which he was going to do. No matter what anyone said.

Alex picked up the pocketknife from the nightstand and pried out the flat-head screwdriver attachment. Then, huddling near the side table, he set about carefully removing the back of the watch.

"Maybe we should just let the Shadow Conjurer win," he muttered. "Maybe that's what both worlds deserve.

"Mom and Dad wanted me to find the Eye. I'm sure of it. But nobody's going to give me a chance. Between Uncle Mordo and Derren I've ended up stuck in a fishing village with rabbit people, fixing watches.

"The Eye," Alex gasped. "I have the Eye. It was inside my dad's watch the entire time!"

Alex had to put the pebble down before his shaking hand dropped it on the floor. Was it actually the Eye? Could it be? He took his parents' journal from his rear pocket and flipped through the pages. There! It matched the sketch perfectly!

He was holding the Eye of Dedi in his hands.

He had to admit that the real thing was much less intriguing than the drawing in the journal. This was just a rock. It didn't look any different from the ones that used to get stuck in his shoe whenever he ran across the gravel drive at Uncle Mordo's.

How did it work? Or did it even work at all? He pinched the pebble, then gingerly tapped it on the nightstand. Nothing happened.

Alex slumped on the bed, staring at the pebble between his fingers. He had the Eye. But he didn't know what to do with it.

Did he have to switch it on or something?

Would Derren know what to do with the thing?

Could it really defeat the Shadow Conjurer? Keep Alex and his sister safe? Bring magic back to the Conjurian?

And why had his parents left him the map coordinates on the pocketknife if the Eye had been in the watch all along?

That last question stuck in Alex's head. Yes, why? He thought hard, and the answer came.

His parents, believing he and Emma would be safe with Uncle Mordo, had hidden the Eye in the watch. They'd assumed that Alex would find it. But they must have known he'd need directions about how to make it work.

That must be what the map coordinates would lead him to! Directions on how to use the Eye!

As soon as Derren and Pimawa got back, Alex would show them the Eye. He'd explain about the coordinates. They'd understand at last.

Alex jumped up and hurried to the window to see if he could catch a glimpse of the platform where the Choosing ceremony would be held. Had the ceremony started? When would Derren and Pimawa and Emma be back?

But what he saw made him realize that he had no time to wait for the others.

Three black specks were in the sky over the ocean, drifting toward Plomboria.

CHAPTER 9

EMMA

As the preparations wound up onstage, Emma noticed a young Jimjarian making his way down the aisle toward their row. She recognized Jukstra, one of the three Jimjarians who'd met Gertie when she'd arrived at the docks.

"Madame Flarraj!" Jukstra whispered loudly when he arrived. "We have an emergency on the docks. We're over capacity and the ships are still arriving."

"Yes, well," said Madame Flarraj, shifting in her seat. "Too many guests are never a problem! We shall have to—"

"Madame Flarraj," said Jukstra, "they are not here for the ceremony. They are fleeing Conjurian City. They're all saying the Tower has fallen."

Her mouth opening and closing, the Conjurian elder looked from Jukstra to Derren, then to Rowlfin and back to Jukstra.

"Perhaps you will believe us now," Derren said, turning to the Jimjarian elder. "Call a halt to the Choosing ceremony, Madame Flarraj. You have more important things to deal with."

Madame Flarraj looked outraged. "Call a halt to the ceremony! Certainly not! We shall welcome all guests. Jimjarians are famous for our hospitality. But the ceremony must go on. That is without question. . . ."

Her voice trailed off as she noticed Jukstra, who was staring at the sky with a glazed look in his eyes.

Emma followed the young Jimjarian's gaze. High above, she could make out three black shapes, like demonic kites, flying straight at the main stage.

Emma knew at once what those shapes must be. Skeletons in fluttering black robes, creatures of the Shadow Conjurer. Rag-O-Rocs. Hunting for her. Her and her brother.

The stage erupted in chaos. As Derren and Rowlfin and Madame Flarraj stared, horror-stricken, Pimawa pulled Emma up and out of her seat, into the mass of Jimjarians fleeing the platform, heading for the elevators.

Emma tried to shake herself free. "Pimawa, let me go! Not this way!"

"We must go this way, Miss Emma!" Pimawa held tightly. "We must get you away from this platform. You're much too exposed here. They'll spot you instantly."

"I know! That's what I want!" Emma twisted her arm loose. "Get away from here! Get everyone else away! They'll chase me!"

She ran in the opposite direction, forcing her way through the mass of fleeing Jimjarians.

"Miss Emma, please!" she heard Pimawa call from behind her back. "That didn't work out so well for your brother!"

"Yeah," said Emma without looking back. "I'm not Alex."

The words sounded brave. But her legs felt hollow, and she was certain her heart would explode any second now. She wasn't sure at all what she was going to do . . . but she knew that if she ran, the Rag-O-Rocs would chase her.

Emma pushed her way free of the last furry body and found herself right before the stage. It was empty now. Derren, Rowlfin, Madame Flarraj, all the Jimjarians—they were gone.

The three Rag-O-Rocs were right above the stage. Emma leaped up onto it. They had to be wondering what she was doing. It looked as if she were running to meet them.

Well, let them wonder.

As the first Rag-O-Roc swooped under the awning, Emma took off across the stage. Ahead was the long dolly on wheels with the two large tubes on it. She made it to the yellow tube and dove in headfirst.

She was safe for the moment . . . but what if the Rag-O-Roc could smell her? Or something?

The tube shook. Emma glimpsed a shadow whisking past the open end—the hem of a tattered black robe. She could only imagine the Rag-O-Roc perched on her tube, pawing at the outside. She wasn't sure how smart the things were. It seemed to know she was in here. Could it figure out a way to get inside?

She felt a lump under one shoulder blade and twisted so she could touch it with her fingers. It felt like a latch. And it brought back a memory. Back in Conjurian City, when the Tower guards had been hot on their trail, Savachia had pushed her inside a wooden box. The bottom had dropped out, and the two of them had fallen into a sewer tunnel. They'd escaped.

It had been a piece of stage illusion, a magic trick. Was this the same thing? She flipped the latch.

A trapdoor slid open, dropping her down into a cramped compartment inside the dolly. The tubes were part of a magic trick after all! The magician's assistant would crawl into one, flip the latch, and drop down into the hiding space.

Then the assistant could probably crawl right underneath the other tube . . . yes! There was a latch here too. It slid open, and Emma wriggled up into the red tube. If she poked her head out, a watcher would think she'd been magically switched from the yellow tube to the red.

Emma inched to one end of the red tube and peered cautiously out. The Rag-O-Roc had thrust its head in the yellow tube and was thrashing around, searching for Emma inside. Stealthily, Emma slid out of the red tube and crawled on her

belly to a table only a few feet away. The table was draped with a black cloth, and if she could get underneath that . . .

A frustrated screech came from behind her, and the yellow tube sailed over her head. The Rag-O-Roc had seen her! The tube missed Emma but hit the table. The brightly colored trunk sitting on it, large enough to hold a person, toppled to the floor. The lid sprang open.

Emma rolled into the trunk. It was longer inside than it appeared. She yanked the lid shut. Surely there would be another trick compartment in here. A latch . . . a trapdoor . . . a hinge . . . In total darkness, she flailed about. Her hands felt nothing but smooth wood.

The lid of the trunk was heaved open and light flooded in. The Rag-O-Roc's bony hands seized Emma's leg. Its head shot inside the box, an angry hiss coming from its empty skull.

Emma kicked wildly, freed her leg, and bent both knees up against her chest. The Rag-O-Roc stabbed its head at her. She punched at its empty eye socket and missed, smashing her hand against the side of the trunk.

A mirrored panel swung down from the trunk's lid, landing hard on the Rag-O-Roc's spine. It thrashed and hissed louder. In the mirror Emma glimpsed a huddled, terrified girl. A surge of hot anger rose up inside Emma. Why was that girl just sitting there, looking so helpless? Why didn't she run—fight—do *something*? Why was she letting other people decide what happened to her?

The girl in the mirror now looked just as angry as Emma.

Emma snapped both legs straight and kicked the Rag-O-Roc smack in the face.

Its head snapped off its neck and bounced across the stage. The rest of the body slumped into the trunk next to Emma.

Shuddering, Emma clambered out of the trunk. She scanned the stage. No sign of the other two Rag-O-Rocs.

Her gaze fell back to the trunk, now full of bones and black tatters.

"So, you can be stopped," Emma said softly. She slapped the lid shut.

A hiss overhead made her head jerk up.

Another Rag-O-Roc perched on the awning over her head, peering in at Emma through a rent in the bright canvas. Its head bobbed from her to its fallen comrade.

They seemed to be intelligent, Emma thought. They could learn. This thing had watched what had happened to the first Rag-O-Roc. It wasn't going to rush in carelessly.

She backed away slowly, then bolted for the elevators.

The Rag-O-Roc vaulted off the awning and soared almost lazily overhead.

Okay. She couldn't outrun it on foot. Eventually it would catch her. But she'd taken out that first one because it had been forced to crawl into the trunk after her.

So she needed a tight, enclosed space. Then she might have a chance.

Emma reached the elevators as the Rag-O-Roc swooped lower. She vaulted into one of the barrels and scanned the stage before releasing the brake.

The Rag-O-Roc hovered above her, sinking as the elevator descended. It wasn't attacking. It was moving closer, slowly, fluttering from one side to another, as if trying to keep her corralled in the elevator.

Why would it *want* to keep her in the elevator? Unless . . .

The third Rag-O-Roc swung down from the ropes holding the elevator and dug its claws into Emma's shoulder. The two monsters were working as a team—and Emma had been herded into an ambush.

As the Rag-O-Roc dragged at her, trying to pull her out of the barrel, Emma snatched at the rope attached to the brake

lever and coiled it
around her arm.

The Rag-O-Roc
tugged, hard. Pain stabbed at her
shoulder where its claws had
taken hold. The rope pulled hard
at one arm, the Rag-O-Roc
yanked at her shoulder, and Emma
felt as if she'd be torn in two any
moment.

With a frustrated hiss, the
beast repositioned itself, skitter-
ing down onto the edge of the
barrel. One hand kept its grip on
Emma's shoulder. The other
reached for the rope.

If it got the rope loose it would
have her, and hoist her away through
the sky. With a surge of adrenaline,
Emma shook the rope off her free
hand and grabbed at the Rag-O-
Roc's wrist. She twisted so that she
could clasp the creature's arm with both hands,
ignoring the pain in her shoulder, and flung herself to the
bottom of the barrel.

Now that the rope was freed, the barrel shot upward. The
Rag-O-Roc, still perched on the edge, tried to shake itself
loose. Emma held tight to its arm as they rocketed higher.
Hang on, she told herself. *Hang on one second more. . . .*

Bones splintered, clattering down the shaft. The elevator jolted to a halt. Emma gasped, still clinging to one skeleton arm. Slowly she got to her feet, her heart hammering, her shoulder throbbing. She had done it! She had beaten two Rag-O-Rocs!

Emma tossed the arm over the side of the barrel and looked down to see it fall. What she actually saw was the third beast soaring up after her.

The elevator could go no higher. It had dumped her onto what appeared to be a maintenance deck above the stage. She heaved herself out of the barrel and stumbled all the way to the edge of the deck. The end of the line.

Below her she saw the stage, swimming in and out of focus. Beyond that was the greenish blur of the water far, far below. Her breathing grew shallow. Dizziness threatened to toss her over the side.

She slipped to her knees. If she fell now, she'd do the Rag-O-Roc's work for it.

The thing had almost made it up to her level. Emma blinked, trying to think clearly, and her gaze focused on the thick metal cables that had been strung from the edge of this deck to the awning over the stage. Red paper lanterns swung from them.

The Rag-O-Roc swooped up, level with the deck. It hovered, its skull face turning from side to side. It had to know she was trapped, but it also seemed aware of what had happened to the last two Rag-O-Rocs that had tried to capture Emma.

The creature drifted closer. It would be in striking distance in a few seconds. It would grab her and carry her back over the sea, back to the Shadow Conjurer. And what could Emma do about it?

Only one thing. And it was ten times scarier than the approaching monster.

The Rag-O-Roc released a shrill cry. Emma let out her breath in one quick puff and swiveled to swing her legs out over the edge of the deck.

She grabbed with both hands at the nearest metal cable. It had more give than she anticipated. Her weight lurched forward and she slid off the ledge. She dropped with a scream, hanging on for dear life.

Emma swung her legs up and hooked them around the cable, bobbing sixty feet over the stage. She slid, stopping at the first lantern. She would have to release her legs to get around it. No way. Not happening!

There was a chittering noise above her. Craning her neck back, she got an upside-down view of the Rag-O-Roc's head peering over the edge of the deck. What was it waiting for? It could easily swoop down and grab her.

But she wasn't going to make its job easy.

Holding her breath, she released her legs and shimmied

past the first lantern. Then she hooked her ankles back over the cable. Only nineteen more till she reached the awning.

Inch by inch, lantern by lantern, she made her way down! Five more lanterns. Four more. She didn't know what the Rag-O-Roc was doing above her. She just had to get down as quickly as she could.

The cord suddenly wobbled violently. Emma's hands slipped loose, and terror gripped her as she swung from her knees, upside down over the stage. The Rag-O-Roc was shaking the cable!

She flailed with both arms and got one hand back on the cable. Then the second. But her hands were sweating with fear and felt slippery on the metal surface. If she tried to move, she'd fall.

If the Rag-O-Roc shook the cable again, she'd fall.

If she just hung here, she'd lose the strength in her hands, and she'd fall.

She was going to fall.

Then she heard a twanging snap. The Rag-O-Roc had snipped the cord.

The wind rushed over her back as she swung down toward the stage. Clamping her eyes shut, she waited for the impact. It never came.

There was a swoop like Emma had felt in the past when a roller coaster had hit the lowest point of its plunge and was starting to climb up again. Opening her eyes, she saw that she had swung past the platform and out over the water.

Below her was nothing but two hundred feet of air. Gripping tight, Emma held her breath as the cable swung her like a pendulum back toward the platform with the stage. And

there was Pimawa, waiting for her, reaching out
over the railing to catch her.

She smiled. Of course Pimawa was there
for her. And then he wasn't.

The cable snapped. The world
blurred past. How long would
she fall? How much
would it hurt when
she wasn't falling
any longer?

CHAPTER 10

ALEX

When Alex reached the docks, the space was packed shoulder to shoulder, making progress almost impossible. As Alex shoved his way into the throng, he noticed that most of the crowd were Conjurians, not Jimjarians.

Alex squeezed his way to the edge and looked out over the water. The sight was unreal. Boats lined the docks so close together they scraped against one another. The bay was clogged with more, every one overcrowded with people and belongings.

Larger vessels had dropped anchor far out in the bay, and a wave of dinghies rowed toward Plomboria.

These were people who'd fled the fall of Conjurian City,

Alex realized. How could he get a ship *off* the island when everybody else was looking to come *onto* it?

Gertie. He needed Neil and Clive and Gertie. Alex pushed on until he saw the uniquely rounded shape of the Grubians' carriage bobbing in the water.

"Gertie!" said Alex. "Am I glad to see you." He waved at the mechanical alpaca as he jumped onto the carriage's roof.

"Neil! Clive!" He banged on the hatch. No answer. He banged again. Still no answer.

Alex cranked the wheel that held the latch closed. It spun easily, and the hatch popped open. Maybe he didn't need Neil and Clive after all. Maybe he only needed their alpaca.

Could he pilot this thing? Of course he could. Tossing the map tube into the opening, Alex swung his legs inside as a voice called from the dock.

"Is this how you repay us for getting you away from Conjurian City? By stealing our vessel? My, my, only a few days in the Conjurian and already turning into a pirate."

"Neil!" Alex flushed at the sight of the stumpy man tapping his foot on the dock. "No! Not at all. I mean I . . . I need your help . . . again. Listen. I have someplace I need to go."

"Without your sister?" Neil stood on the edge of the dock, his arms laden with a crate full of assorted baked goods. "Or your Jimjarian? Or Master Derren himself?"

"Yes," said Alex. "Emma will be safe here. They'll all be safe here. But we have to hurry. I can fill you in once we get going."

"If your sister will be safe *here* . . . hmmm." Neil shook his head. "That implies your destination is dangerous, which in turn precludes us from being involved."

Neil's brother emerged from the crowd. He carried a stack of boxes, blocking his vision. "Clive!" Neil called out, setting the boxes at his feet. "Would you mind escorting the younger Maskelyne back to—"

Alex leaped down onto the dock next to Clive. He pulled his father's watch from his pocket and clicked the lid open to reveal the small rock resting on the watch's face.

"I have the Eye of Dedi." He said it loud and enunciated every word. He wanted everyone nearby to hear. He had to make sure that

everyone knew he was in possession of the Eye. That way the Shadow Conjurer would pursue him. Emma could remain here, safe and sound.

Neil dropped the crate and roughly pulled Alex close, clamping the watch shut. "Are you mad? You don't yell things like that in public. 'Fire' in a crowded theater, sure, but not 'I have the most powerful relic in magic history.'" Neil relaxed his grip and stared at Alex. "How can you be sure that's the Eye?"

"It matches the sketches in my parents' journal," said Alex. "They hid it with me all this time, and then they led the Shadow Conjurer on a wild goose chase. They did it all to save us. I'm going to do the same."

"How does it work?" asked Neil eagerly.

"I don't know!" Alex shoved the watch into his pocket. "Look, my parents hid some map coordinates on a knife they left for me. I brought the chart that can get us to those coordinates. But there are Rag-O-Rocs on the way! I have to get out of here WITH THE EYE OF DEDI!" Alex shouted the last five words as loudly as he could.

Neil clamped his greasy palm over Alex's mouth. "What is wrong with you? Hush!"

Too late. There was no mistaking the growing murmur around them. Heads were starting to turn.

Humans and Jimjarians glanced at their companions with questioning looks and then pointed.

But they weren't pointing at Alex.

Everyone was gazing out into the bay where three bony, black-robed figures burst out of a bank of cloud.

The dock erupted in chaos. Some people tried to reboard their boats while others scrambled to get off. Neil was staring in shock at the approaching creatures; Clive dropped his load of boxes on his own toes.

Alex felt despair close in on him. It was too late for his plan to divert the Shadow Conjurer's attention away from Plomboria, away from Emma and Derren and Pimawa. Or was it?

Alex darted away from Neil, who shook himself out of his trance soon enough to make a grab for the fleeing boy, but not soon enough to catch him. Alex leaped onto one of the wooden cranes used to unload the fishing boats and started to climb.

Once he was above the heads of most of the people on the dock, he stopped climbing and waved one hand furiously. "Hey! Boneheads! Down here! Look what I have! I have the Eye! Come and get it!"

But it was no use. He was yelling at the top of his lungs, but the Rag-O-Rocs did not seem to hear. They seemed to have focused their attention on something high up on the other column and were soaring that way without a glance at what was happening below.

He was about to climb higher when two long arms wrapped around his legs and pulled him from the crane. He looked down into Clive Grubian's expressionless face. "Hey!" Alex shouted angrily. "Let me go!"

Clive hoisted him back to the carriage and dumped him onto the dock. Neil clamped a hand around his wrist.

"What are you doing?" asked Alex, twisting and pulling his wrist to no avail. "We have to help Emma."

Neil picked Alex up and swung him out over the hatch in the carriage's roof. "Time to go, my boy." He let go, and Alex fell heavily into the interior of the carriage, landing on a bean-bag chair.

"What? No, I can't go now, not until Emma is safe!" Alex tried climbing out. Neil's scuffed shoe pushed his face, knocking him back down.

"Don't you worry," said Neil, climbing down after him with the map canister under one arm. "Won't need this. We already know exactly where we're taking you."

EMMA

Emma stopped falling with a thump. But it didn't hurt half as much as she expected. She was cradled in a stretchy trampoline of red and green stripes. The awning! She'd landed on the awning over the stage! Maybe she'd survive this after all. . . .

The awning ripped, sending her down once more, somersaulting in a shroud of red and green.

She landed hard, which knocked the wind out of her. Entangled in the remnants of the awning, she rolled down a slope—a ramp of some kind? Then the cloth ripped away and she saw that she was on a roof tiled with clamshells. She was only on it for a short time, however, because she promptly fell off.

All Emma could picture was the time Alex had made a parachute for one of her dolls and tossed it off the fourth-floor balcony, then watched it smash against the marble floor. The doll had had a more successful flight than she was having at the present moment.

As she fell, she saw flashes of water, horrified Jimjarian faces, roofs, railings. She caught one last streak of blue before the third impact.

This one wasn't as hard or as wet as she had expected. In fact, it was soft. She lay still for a moment, her eyes clamped shut, afraid the slightest movement would send her tumbling once more. But nothing seemed to be happening. After a moment she cautiously moved each limb. Despite an ache in her left leg and the throbbing in her right shoulder, nothing seemed broken.

Her back prickled. She blinked her eyes open, only to stare at a mass of color—pink, purple, scarlet, yellow, white. Everything around her felt sharp and soft at the same time. The aroma reminded her of Uncle Mordo's gardens.

She sat up and shook her head, and blossoms spilled over her like water. She'd landed on a barge full of flowers, probably meant to decorate Plomboria for the Choosing ceremony. She spat out what looked like a spotted lily before releasing a cry of joy.

A crowd gawked from the packed dock next to the barge. Many were staring up at the sky, as if expecting another young girl to fall. Emma stood. She brushed the leaves and petals from her pants and, limping a little, made her way to the side of the boat.

Screams erupted from the dock. People and Jimjarians dove for the water as the third Rag-O-Roc bounded over their heads and landed on the barge's bow. The ship rocked. Emma edged backward, looking behind her to see the terrified captain peeking out of the pilothouse window.

The Rag-O-Roc hissed, lunging forward. Emma slipped on the slick plants and fell on her back. She rolled sideways off the mound of greenery and smashed into the railing around the barge's deck. Looking for cover, she noticed the black webbing of a net hanging over the side.

The Rag-O-Roc snarled at her from atop the mound, struggling to get its footing on the crushed blossoms and slippery leaves. It wasn't letting its prey escape again. With a roar that could shatter crystal, it jumped for her.

Emma seized the heavy net and spun, whipping it up over the side of the barge. The other end of the net flared open and wrapped around the Rag-O-Roc.

Off balance and confused, the Rag-O-Roc fell, and the net carried the entangled creature over the side of the barge and right into the water. It sank fast. Bubbles erupted at the surface. Emma leaned on the railing, watching and waiting to see if the beast would surface.

It didn't.

Emma stared at the water in amazement. Something was dawning on her.

She was only a kid, and she'd just smashed three Rag-O-Rocs. Kicked the head off one, crushed another in an elevator, and knocked the final one into the ocean.

These were the things that had taken down Conjurian City, and they were not all that hard to kill.

"I fought them," she said, dazed.

"You sure did," a voice agreed.

She looked up to see Savachia on the dock, looking impressed.

"I thought you might need a hand," he said, offering her one. "Getting over to

the dock, I mean. You seem to have dealt with everything else just fine."

Emma reached out automatically and took his hand. Her legs felt wobbly, and she was glad for the support as she jumped off the barge and onto the dock.

Faces were staring at her. Some human, some Jimjarian. All amazed.

"There might be more of those things coming," Savachia said quietly in her ear. "Better get you somewhere safe."

"No."

Emma said it softly, but then she repeated it more loudly. "No more hiding."

She'd fought three Rag-O-Rocs and won.

Everyone had kept telling her not to fight. That she had no chance. That the Shadow Conjurer was far too powerful. She'd believed them. She'd accepted that the only thing to do was get away. Run. Hide.

But they were wrong. Alex—Pimawa—Derren— Madame Flarraj. They were all wrong.

The Rag-O-Rocs looked terrifying, sure. But they weren't invincible. They were even kind of—she almost laughed at the thought—fragile.

A magic trunk, an elevator, and a fishing net were all it had taken to knock three Rag-O-Rocs out of the game. Why would the Shadow Conjurer use these creatures as his soldiers, unless he couldn't come up with anything better?

Unless he was a lot less powerful than everyone believed?

CHAPTER 11

ALEX

Inside the carriage, balanced against the gentle rocking that Gertie was making as she paddled out to sea, Neil Grubian held the Eye between his thumb and forefinger. "Very careless for someone so bright. Running off into the great unknown. You and the Eye would have vanished forever. Such a waste."

Alex swiped at the Eye, but Neil tossed it over his shoulder to Clive.

"So you believe it has power?" asked Neil, eyeing Alex with a hint of a smile on his face. "I thought you didn't believe in magic at all—yet you seem to want this trinket very badly."

Frustration and rage were forcing hot tears into Alex's

eyes. He blinked them back. He needed time to come up with an escape—and he needed to get the Eye back in his hands.

"It's only a rock," said Alex. "*You* obviously want it badly enough to kidnap me so you can get your hands on it. You kidnap me, Savachia kidnaps Emma . . . is kidnapping the national pastime in the Conjurian or something?"

"Oh, gracious." Neil stepped back, looking hurt. "Clive, we have frightened our young friend. Yes, I can see how one might perceive this as a kidnapping. However . . ." Neil winked. "Think of me as a pudgy little genie rather than an abductor. I'm going to give you what you always wanted. Answers. Knowledge, my boy! Good deal, yes?" Neil smiled wider. The smile vanished. "There is a slight downside. We can't guarantee you'll survive."

Clive tossed the Eye back to Alex.

Alex snatched it out of the air, relief making him woozy for a moment. But the relief drained away as quickly as it had come. Whether he had the Eye in his hands or not, he was still at the Grubians' mercy.

"Where are you taking me?" Alex asked.

"To someone who knows how the Eye works, or at least thinks he does." Neil snapped his fingers. Clive brought over a tea tray and set it down in front of Alex.

"We can fill you in on the ride," said Neil. "I can't remember, do you take sugar?" Without waiting for an answer, Neil handed Alex a cup.

Alex shoved his hand away, spilling hot tea all over the tray. Neil moved neatly aside to avoid being scalded.

The smaller Grubian brother was much quicker on his feet than you might think to look at him. And smarter too. In fact, Alex was starting to believe that very little of what he'd thought about Neil and Clive Grubian was true.

He'd thought that the brothers were smugglers. Performers. Con men, probably. Untrustworthy for sure.

But he hadn't thought of them as masterminds.

Alex remembered the way the brothers had burst onto the scene when he and Emma and Pimawa had just arrived in the Conjurian. The three of them had been lost in the Mysts, about to be devoured by a wolf-headed snake. Neil and Clive's sudden arrival had frightened off the creature and saved them.

Such a lucky coincidence. Or . . . not?

"You didn't find us in the Mysts by chance, did you?" he said slowly, thinking aloud. "You were looking for us!"

"Well, there you go, Clive." Neil picked up broken shards of teacup from the carriage's floor. "A regular virtuoso of deduction. I was wondering how long it would take you to figure that out. To be fair, you have been a bit distracted."

"How did you know we'd be there?"

"We have many sources," said Neil. "Magicians are surprisingly bad at keeping secrets. There was a sizable bounty on the Maskelyne children if they showed up in the Conjurian, you know—or perhaps you don't. No matter. We jumped at the employment opportunity, not knowing at the time who the employer was. But as fate would have it, your sister slipped out of our grasp in Conjurian City, and you were hauled off to the Tower yourself. Then we found sweet young Emma again—or, rather, she found us. Then you found each other. And now we've lost her but we have you. And the Eye." Neil frowned as if slightly confused, then nodded. "Yes, that's about right. So, we turn you in for half the bounty."

"You work for the Shadow Conjurer!" said Alex. Rage bubbled up in him. He hadn't exactly liked Neil and Clive, he hadn't exactly trusted them . . . but he hadn't thought they were working for anyone but themselves.

"Wizz-wow, Clive!" Neil clapped as he spun on his heels. "Sharp as a cleaver, this one."

Alex wanted to hit him. To pummel him to a pulp. But he forced his anger down. Anger wasn't going to help him here.

Logic might.

"Wait. What about the Eye?" asked Alex. "Aren't you going to turn that over to him? He only wants me to get to the Eye. If you give the Eye to him, I bet the reward will be even bigger."

"Alas . . ." Neil laid a hand to his forehead. "We could only enjoy that larger reward right until the Shadow Conjurer destroyed the world. In our business it's always wise to keep your best card up your sleeve. No, we'll enjoy the bounty we earn from handing you over, and we'll save the Eye for a stormier day."

Alex scowled. "What if I tell him you have it?"

"Ah, yes, there is that," said Neil. "In a game of chess, Master Maskelyne, you must always be several moves ahead of your opponent."

"I could beat you any day at chess."

"That may be true." Neil's grin spread all the way across his ample face. "However, in our game, not all of the pieces make the moves that you might expect."

EMMA

Emma grabbed Savachia's arm to steady herself. She turned to the humans and Jimjarians on the dock.

"Listen," she croaked out. She could barely hear herself! This wouldn't do.

"Listen! Everyone! I know a lot of you must be from Conjurian City. You've all seen what the Shadow Conjurer can do."

There was a murmur of fear at the mention of the dreaded name. People began to shuffle back along the dock, away from Emma.

"But you don't get it! He's a *fraud*!"

Emma yelled this last word as loudly as she could.

"He's nothing! Look at what just happened. I smashed three of his Rag-O-Rocs. Three! They look scary, but we can beat them. We can, if we fight together!"

Everybody was staring blankly at her. A few people were muttering anxiously. Nobody looked convinced.

"I'm telling you, the Rag-O-Rocs can be beaten!" Emma shouted, her voice rising with frustration. "The Shadow Conjurer can be beaten! Why aren't you listening? What's *wrong* with you?"

Savachia's hand clamped around her arm.

"Insulting people is very rarely a good way to make them do what you want," he said in her ear.

"Fine!" Emma swung around to glare at him. "But you know I'm right! Can't you see it? I was right all along. The Shadow Conjurer *can* be beaten. He's nothing but a big bully, hiding behind his toy monsters. We don't have to run from him!"

"You're asking people to risk their lives," Savachia pointed out. The crowd on the dock had started to move on. Most of them were ignoring Emma and Savachia completely. "You can't yell at people and make them do something like that. You have to persuade them."

"Fine." Emma crossed her arms and glared. "You do it."

"Me?" Savachia blinked, genuinely amazed.

"Yeah, you. It's what you do, isn't it? Persuade people?"

"Con them. Isn't that what you mean? I'm a con man, remember?"

"Yeah, I remember." Emma softened her voice a little. "I also remember how you conned me into trusting you."

Savachia looked a little guilty.

"I know why you did it. To save your dad. Well, how about doing it again? To save the world this time? And I'll make sure you get something out of it."

Savachia raised an eyebrow. "Oh yeah? Like what?"

"Like the Eye of Dedi."

She'd actually shocked Savachia into speechlessness. That must be a first.

"Alex thinks he knows where to find the Eye," Emma told him. "If he's right . . . then I'll make sure you get your hands on it. You can use it to save your mom."

"And if he's wrong?" Savachia asked skeptically.

"Then you'll still be helping to save the world. There isn't actually a downside here."

To her amazement, Savachia laughed. Then he reached out, snatched a silver ball and a scarf from a basket that a passing Jimjarian was carrying, and jumped off the dock. He landed squarely on the barge full of flowers.

Savachia waded through the flowers and leaped up onto the roof of the cabin. The captain's head popped out of a window and he began to berate the boy, but Savachia ignored him.

He tossed the silver ball up, stretched the scarf, and caught the ball on the edge of the fabric. It balanced there as if on a tabletop.

"Good morning!" he shouted to the crowd on the deck as they turned to look at his magic trick. "Greetings on this fine day! Or not so fine day, I suppose, for those of you who have come here from Conjurian City. For those of you who've seen the Shadow Conjurer face to face."

Fear clouded the faces looking up at him. Some people and Jimjarians backed away or started to walk faster, but some seemed surprised enough to stay and listen.

"I want to introduce you to someone. To this young lady here!" Savachia gestured at Emma. "She, too, has seen the Shadow Conjurer. And she has shown more bravery in the past couple of days than the Circle has in decades. She charged headlong into the Tower to confront the Shadow Conjurer— with my help, of course. Alas, the two of us were lucky to get out alive. But there is no doubt, with the proper forces behind her, Emma Maskelyne will defeat our common enemy. Who can argue with me? Who here did not see what she just did? The first three Rag-O-Rocs to invade Plomboria fell by her hand!"

Emma felt herself blushing furiously. The people who'd been listening to Savachia were turning to look at her. Most of them seemed doubtful.

"Now, you may say this young lady is a heroine." Savachia grinned as Emma blushed hotter. "But me? I'm no hero, I promise you that. No, I'm in this for myself. All of you should be in this for yourselves!"

What was he saying? Emma turned to Savachia, worried. He was supposed to be inspiring everybody to fight, not telling them to be selfish.

Savachia paid Emma no heed. The ball rolled gently along the edge of the scarf and then dropped behind it. "For too long we have all whispered the Shadow Conjurer's name. Fooling ourselves that if we didn't say it too loud, he wouldn't come. Guess what? He came to Conjurian City!"

"You got that right, kid!" called a voice from the crowd.

From behind the scarf, the ball pushed at the cloth. Savachia stroked it, as if taming it, and it eased back. "He tore down the Tower of Dedi. Wait—I meant his army of Rag-O-Rocs shredded it."

Startled murmuring erupted among the onlookers. Emma wanted to strangle Savachia. First he'd told them to look after themselves, and now he was trying to scare them?

Savachia twisted the scarf around. The ball was gone! It peeked over his shoulder and he snatched it up and dropped it back behind the scarf. "Yeah, that's right. Rag-O-Rocs. They're real too. You've seen them, some of you. They're more real than this!"

Savachia dropped the scarf, revealing the ball in his hands. It was supported by a black rod with a loop on one end that he had slipped around his middle finger. While the ball had seemed to be floating on the edge of the scarf or drifting about behind it, he'd been holding it in place himself.

Savachia jabbed the rod toward the crowd. "More Rag-O-Rocs are coming. And Emma won't be here to save you from all of them. Because she's taking the fight to the Shadow Conjurer himself. And me, I'm with her." He tossed the ball

to Emma, who caught it on reflex. "I'm with her because she's the only one who has ever stood up and said enough is enough. It's time to stop whispering his name and join Emma to finish the Shadow Conjurer once and for all!"

Emma was amazed. She felt like jumping up and down and cheering herself. She felt ready to fight a legion of Rag-O-Rocs. She swung to face the crowd, beaming.

No one was beaming back.

A few people were nodding. A few were talking urgently to their companions. But no one was rushing to her side. No one was waving a hand in the air, eager to volunteer.

"So . . . if you want to . . . ," she said hesitatingly. Her voice was much weaker than Savachia's. She cleared her throat. "Right now. We just need some of these boats, and we can . . ."

Savachia jumped off the cabin roof, saluted the captain, and leaped onto the dock.

"Give them time," he said quietly to Emma.

"Time?" She turned to stare at him. "Time is the one thing we don't have! More Rag-O-Rocs could be here any minute. We've got to get moving!"

"Armies don't form in an hour," Savachia said. "But look at them. They're talking. They're thinking. I planted a seed, and that's all you can do at the start. Let's get back to Rowlfin's house," he said, raising his voice. "That's where she'll be. If anyone wants to talk about fighting and not running, that's where to find us!"

CHAPTER 12

EMMA

Savachia and Emma trudged all the way back to Rowlfin's house. At least Emma found that the elevators and the bridge did not frighten her anymore.

So that was one good thing.

But it was the only good thing she could think of. The people hadn't listened to her. They hadn't really listened to Savachia.

Savachia could talk all he wanted to about planting seeds, about first steps, about going slowly . . . but Emma knew failure when she saw it. The Jimjarians and the Conjurian refugees were not going to fight.

Once they reached the gate of Rowlfin's house, Pimawa rushed out. "Oh, Miss Emma! Praise Dedi! You're alive!"

He flung his furry arms around her and she hugged back. It felt comforting, a little.

But his next words took the comfort away entirely.

"Miss Emma, have you seen your brother?"

A few minutes later, Emma and Savachia and Pimawa stared in shock at the note on the table.

Em,
 I found the Eye. It was hidden in Dad's busted watch all this time. I'm going on my expedition to find a way to beat the Shadow Conjurer. Before I leave, I'll make sure everyone knows I have the Eye. That way, he'll come after me. You'll be safe in Plomboria.
 When I find answers, I'll come back. Then we can fight the Shadow Conjurer together. Stay safe.
  Stay out of sight. I will see you soon.

Love,
 Alex
P.S. Please tell Pimawa I was starting to like him.

"Where is he? Where's he gone?" Emma looked up, wide-eyed, at Pimawa.

"We do not know. Down to the docks, we assume. But it's chaos down there. Refugees from the Conjurian are arriving."

"Yeah, we know." Savachia nodded.

"Master Derren and my father are searching for him— and you. Now that you've come back, Miss Emma, I will join them. Please stay here. If your brother returns, make him stay as well."

Emma stared numbly at the note. She nodded.

"I'll go too," Savachia said quietly, getting up from the table. "I've been checking out this city since I got here. There are a few places I can search for him."

Emma sat at the table, looking at her brother's note, while Pimawa and Savachia rushed out. She stared at the letter, thinking hard.

They weren't going to find Alex. She knew it. When Alex made a plan, it worked. He'd figured out some way to get what he wanted, so he was gone.

When he returned, he would be expecting to find her here, in Plomboria. Hiding. Safe. Her brother had become just another person telling her to do nothing.

Well, she wasn't going to.

If Alex could take off on his own quest, so could she.

If the Jimjarians and the Conjurians were not going to fight the Shadow Conjurer, then it was up to Emma.

She stood up, leaving Alex's note on the table, and marched out of the house.

Alex climbed out of the hatch on top of the carriage. Clive followed behind, gripping the wire handles of two lanterns in his teeth. He handed one lantern to Neil, who climbed out third and hopped from foot to foot around the hatch.

"Close now, oh so close," said Neil.

Alex remained on all fours. His stomach lurched as the carriage rose higher out of the black water. They had resurfaced inside a subterranean cavern. Gertie guided the carriage to the rocky shore. When they reached the water's edge, her paddles transformed back into legs and she hauled the carriage onto jagged land.

Clive lit the lanterns, illuminating the deep purple stone surrounding them.

Alex swallowed his fear. The only thing that could help him now was more information. Facts. Knowledge. "Are we under the city?" he asked, steadying himself against Clive as the carriage jerked to a stop. "Conjurian City?"

"Indeed we are, my boy. You're starting to put it all together." Neil tapped his temple.

The last time Alex had seen Conjurian City, he'd been fleeing for his life. The Tower had been torn down, the Shadow Conjurer had killed Christopher Agglar and taken over, and Rag-O-Rocs had been pursuing Alex and his friends through the streets.

He'd never wanted to return. But here he was.

Clive jumped down onto a narrow, pebbled shore along the water's edge. A ladder unfolded itself from a slot in the carriage's side, and Clive steadied it for Alex and his brother as they climbed down.

Neil and Clive held their lanterns high, which, for Neil, wasn't very high at all. The splotchy yellow light revealed a narrow sliver of rocky ground that led up to a black hole in the cave wall.

"Shall we?" Neil slapped Alex on the back.

"What's in there?" Alex pointed at the opening.

"Answers to be discovered, not told." Neil plodded toward the opening. "Here, I'll go first."

"What part of the city are we under? I'm guessing we must be close to the Tower." Alex followed Neil. With Clive looming at his back, he had little choice. "Why did the Shadow Conjurer want the Tower, anyway? Does it have to do with the gateway between the Flatworld and the Conjurian?"

"As I told you, my little question factory, the answers are this way." Neil extended the lantern, lighting the passage.

Alex shuffled forward. What he saw inside the tunnel sparked his interest enough to subdue his fear—a little bit. The tunnel had been carved by hand. Symbols covered the pale walls.

Alex ran his fingers over the carvings. They were like hieroglyphs. And yet very different.

"Impressive, yes?" asked Neil. He waited a few steps ahead, enjoying Alex's awe. "They are familiar to you?"

"I thought they were Egyptian. They're not." Alex followed the symbols farther into the tunnel. A pattern was emerging. "They're laid out like instructions."

Neil swung his lantern in a slow arc. "Close. Story goes that Dedi built this after arriving in . . . er . . . creating the Conjurian. Take your pick."

"Why?" The burning desire for answers kept Alex moving, despite the fear pulling at his insides.

"Escape route. He feared the Pharaoh would find a way to access the Conjurian and come after him," said Neil.

"Is that why only one official portal between the two

worlds is allowed?" asked Alex. He remembered Pimawa explaining this. One gateway between the two worlds, guarded at all times. One way in and one way out. Unless, of course, you knew where to find one of the secret, private gateways. Neil and Clive knew several, Alex was sure. Successful smugglers would have to.

"Hmph. Perhaps. Who can say?" Neil answered with a shrug. "To be honest, I don't believe Dedi ever wanted other magicians to find this world. I think he wanted a private utopia for his family. Kind of selfish, methinks." Neil stopped. "End of the line. Just through there."

Neil held out his lantern. Another dark opening gaped before Alex.

Alex's tongue stuck to the roof of his mouth. The lantern light swayed back and forth, touching the edge of the opening. It seemed the light didn't want to step out of the tunnel either.

Alex swallowed, feeling an ache in the back of his throat. Was the Shadow Conjurer through there?

Time to find out. Alex took a deep breath and stepped out of the tunnel.

He could not see at first where he had arrived. There was almost no light at all, merely a faint blue luminescence that seemed to hang in the air.

Strong downdrafts made Alex guess the cavern was large, with an opening somewhere above. Shapes that did not appear to be natural rock formations loomed out of the dim blue light. As his eyes adjusted, his jaw slackened.

Those shapes were definitely not natural.

EMMA

Things had calmed down a little at the docks. Only a few boats were still arriving. Emma thought she might be imagining it, but were people looking sideways at her as she passed? Pointing at her and whispering to each other behind her back?

"Fought three of them! Killed them!" she heard one passerby say.

"That girl? She's the one?"

". . . says we ought to . . ."

Emma stood on the dock where Gertie had been moored, but the Grubians' carriage was no longer there. Neil and Clive must have moved it elsewhere. Gertie would have been the fastest way to do what she planned to do—but there were others.

Like the wooden canoe bobbing by the dock, tied by a single line.

She sat down on the edge of the dock and eased herself into the canoe. It rocked and then stabilized as she steadied her weight.

She picked up a paddle and loosened the line holding the canoe to the dock. She shoved off.

"Miss Emma! Miss Emma! What are you doing?" Pimawa came pelting down the dock, heading straight for her.

"Go back, Pimawa! Find Alex!" Emma shouted at him.

Pimawa ignored her. He flexed his powerful hind legs and jumped.

He landed in the canoe behind Emma, very nearly capsizing it. She held back a shriek and dropped her paddle so that she could cling to the gunwales.

"What are you *doing*?" asked Pimawa, shifting his weight to balance the craft. "You and your brother—the minute I turn my back, I lose one or the other of you. We have to get you back into town. Your shoulder—it's injured. We'll have a doctor look at you. Then I'll keep searching for Master Alex."

Emma picked up her paddle from the bottom of the canoe. "No. I'll take you back to the dock. Then I have to get moving."

Pimawa looked horrified. "Absolutely not!"

"Fine, you can get out here." Emma shrugged and faced away from him. She pointed the canoe toward open water and started to paddle.

Pimawa dropped his own paddle and clamped on to the sides. "I am not getting out. What are you planning on doing?"

Emma sighed. "If my brother's still on Plomboria, good.

I don't think he is. He's gone on his quest—and I'm going on mine."

"Then I am going with you." Pimawa joined her in the paddling duties.

"Pim, no. You stay here, with your dad." Emma twisted around, catching the hurt look on his face. "Look, I know it's your duty to protect us, but I can't have you risk your life. What I'm doing is, as Alex would say, an idea so stupid it hurts. I'm already hurt, so I'm halfway there. Stay here. Stay with your family."

"You and Alex are my family," said Pimawa. "And Alex has my father and Master Derren and that Savachia lad to help him right now. I am not going to leave you all alone. Paddle to starboard, Miss Emma."

"Paddle to what?"

"Your right, Miss Emma! Paddle on your right!"

Emma faced forward in time to see a large ferry cutting through the water straight toward them. She paddled on the right. The boat's horn blared as it passed, barely missing them.

The canoe rocked in its wake and slowly steadied.

"I daresay you will need me," said Pimawa.

ALEX

A forest of glass cylinders spread out before Alex. Bolts the size of his fist anchored them to the cavern floor. Each cylinder was capped with a copper lid from which sprouted thick tubes that glowed a faint blue. Some of the tubes were much brighter than others.

Alex was entranced enough to forget, for the moment, about Neil and Clive behind him. To forget that the Shadow Conjurer was waiting for him. He kept moving, winding his way between tubes. They reminded Alex of Gertie's engine, powered by a glowing blue cylinder of stored magical power. This looked sort of the same, except on a massive scale.

Stepping in close to one cylinder, Alex placed his hand on the glass. The nebulous vapor on the other side of the glass gathered around his palm as if attracted to his skin's heat, allowing Alex to see what was inside.

Alex stumbled back, horrified. Christopher Agglar had his faults, but he certainly didn't deserve this.

"Is . . . is he still alive?" Alex looked back. Neil and Clive remained in the tunnel opening. "Everyone here? Are they alive?"

"As much as they can be," said Neil. "Not sure what happens when every drop of magic is drained from a person. Most didn't have much to start with."

Alex stared out at the forest of tubes, slowly beginning to understand what he was looking at.

He'd been right. This was like Gertie's engine. He was looking at the source of the Shadow Conjurer's power: magician upon magician, imprisoned in the cylinders while their magical power was sucked up into the tubes above.

Alex formulated a hypothesis: if you wired together hundreds, maybe thousands of magicians, you'd drain a world of its magic. And you'd have enough power to create an army of Rag-O-Rocs. But eventually you would run out of magicians.

That, Alex realized, was why the Shadow Conjurer needed the Eye. He needed even more power than he was getting from these poor imprisoned people.

Why? What was he planning to do with all that power?

Alex had no idea. But he had to put an end to it, no matter what the cost.

CHAPTER 13

EMMA

Fog hugged the canoe as Emma and Pimawa paddled for what must have been hours through the choppy waters. To Emma's surprise, she heard a chuckle from Pimawa. He tried to turn it into a cough, but it was unmistakable.

"What's so funny?" she asked.

"I do apologize, Miss Emma," said Pimawa. "It merely struck me as ironic. The last instructions your uncle gave you were to follow me—and now it is my turn to follow you. So, given that we are headed toward certain death, what, may I inquire, is the plan?"

Emma wiped the fog from her eyes. She clutched the paddle tightly. The air felt colder as she took a slow breath. "The plan. Right. Well, the Shadow Conjurer went after the Tower of Dedi. There must have been a reason. Alex told me that the Tower is the main connection between my world—the Flatworld—and the Conjurian. That's right?"

"Quite correct, Miss Emma," Pimawa answered.

"He wants the Eye of Dedi—which created this world, split it off from the Flatworld," Emma mused aloud, paddling as she spoke. "And he's got the Tower, which connects both worlds. Derren said he could be planning to destroy the Flatworld and the Conjurian and then re-create them. Rule them both. But if we stop him before he gets the Eye of Dedi, before he gets his hands on Alex, then he can't do that. So the plan is to go to the Tower."

"And then?" Pimawa inquired.

Emma swallowed. "I haven't quite figured that part out yet." The fog had grown so thick that she was certain she

could write her name in it with the paddle. "Pim, are you positive we're going in the right direction?"

"Sure as my ears. I'm a Jimjarian," said Pimawa. "We know these waters well. We'll strike the mainland any moment, and then we simply follow the shore."

They continued paddling in silence for some time, until massive shadows suddenly materialized all around the canoe. Both Emma and Pimawa reflexively raised their paddles, relaxing once they saw they had navigated into a school of

Myst fish. Emma marveled at the beauty of the creatures as they drifted past—huge fish, each the size of a small car, with fins and scales that glimmered a dull silver.

"Are those things everywhere?" asked Emma.

"Everywhere there's mist," said Pimawa.

"You should've stayed behind," said Emma.

"And miss the end of the world? Perish the thought," said Pimawa. "Besides, my duty is to keep you safe, Miss Emma."

"You don't have to follow Uncle Mordo's orders anymore." Emma looked back at Pimawa as the Myst fish drifted slowly away. "And just call me Emma. Or Em. It's weird for friends to use *Miss*."

"Of course, Mi . . . Emma." The pink showed through Pimawa's fur. "And I'm not following Master Mordo's orders. This is what I want to do." Pimawa's ears twisted sharply. He stopped paddling.

"What? What do you hear?" asked Emma, hoping it was another school of Myst fish. She could only hear the water lapping the side of the canoe, but she knew that Pimawa's hearing was much keener than hers.

"Someone approaching. Behind us," Pimawa said softly.

As quietly as they could, Emma and Pimawa steered their craft around to face the approaching threat. Several slender shapes appeared through the mist. Then dozens more.

"He's found us," said Pimawa, quivering enough to rock the boat.

Emma bent forward, raising her paddle. "Then this is where we start fighting back."

ALEX

In the center of the cylinders there was a rough rock column, a natural stalagmite. It stretched up into what used to be the hollow interior of the massive tree that had formed the base of the Tower of Dedi.

The Tower was gone now. All that remained was a stump with about ten feet of crumbling stone wall in a ring around the top. The only opening in that wall was the entrance through which Alex had been marched, in chains, on his first full day in the Conjurian. There he'd paused to watch a magician—Harold the Great, the man had called himself—transit through the portal from the Flatworld.

That portal, the gateway, was still there.

It stood on a platform built into the great stalagmite. A strip of floor about the width of a sidewalk connected the platform to the old entrance. More bits of crumbling floor clung to the stump itself, making a ring around the open space.

All the blue tubes on top of the glass cylinders coiled around the stalagmite and traveled up to the platform. So the Shadow Conjurer was siphoning all the power out of these poor people and channeling it up there? To the gateway? Why?

"Hulloooooo!" Neil's voice echoed into the cavern. "We have come to collect our payment!"

His eyes on the gateway above, Alex didn't notice the Rag-O-Roc until skeletal arms scooped him off the cavern floor. Below, he heard Neil exclaim, "We had a deal!"

The Rag-O-Roc's bony fingers dug into Alex's armpits as it soared straight up above the gateway and then dropped him. Alex fell a good ten feet before slamming into the platform. The wind burst from his lungs. Gasping, trying to regain his breath, he looked up at the robed figure standing over him.

"Welcome, my young skeptic," said the Shadow Conjurer. "You shall have the best seat for the show of shows."

Alex stared up at the bluish face with the three red scars, at the empty eye sockets that made the master of the Rag-O-Rocs look like his skeletal subjects. The last time Alex had seen him, it had been in the hallway of his uncle's mansion, right before Uncle Mordo had kissed him and Emma, told them goodbye, and sent them on their way to the Conjurian.

Uncle Mordo had stayed behind to face the Shadow Conjurer—and died. He'd given up his life so that Emma and Alex could live.

Now Alex had ended up back in the Shadow Conjurer's hands.

The Shadow Conjurer pivoted to the side, revealing a short copper pedestal that stood in front of the gateway. All the glowing blue tubes from below fed into one thicker tube, which was attached to the bottom of this pedestal. On top of the pedestal was a steel ring about as wide as Alex's outstretched hand.

The Shadow Conjurer opened his robe, exposing a metal plate that seemed to have been somehow welded to his chest. In the center of the metal plate was a ring-shaped depression, just the size of the ring on the copper pedestal.

As Alex stared, baffled and horrified, the Shadow Conjurer picked up the steel ring and, with a twist, locked it onto his chest. Blue light rose from the copper pedestal and pulsed into him, trickling around his body in fingers of lightning.

"It is nice to finally be out of the shadows," the Shadow Conjurer said with a smile. "No longer having to hide my power source."

"This isn't magic. This is a crazy man's science experiment," wheezed Alex.

"You're almost correct. It is indeed more science than magic." The Shadow Conjurer laughed. "Look around you. I have nearly drained the last drops of magic from this world. But I still need more. Much, much more."

The Shadow Conjurer stepped closer to Alex. Blue sparks crackled around him. "And you, my little genius, are the key to getting the power I need. You are my way to recover the Eye of Dedi."

So he didn't know. The Shadow Conjurer didn't know that Alex had already found the Eye.

Alex had a secret. That meant Alex had some power. But to use that power, he had to figure out how the Eye worked. Could he make the Shadow Conjurer tell him? Not trusting his aching legs enough to stand, Alex scooted backward. "Agglar tried the same thing. Guess what? Turns out I know nothing about the Eye. I was only two years old when my parents died. They didn't tell me a thing about the Eye. Or the Conjurian. Or much of anything, really."

The Shadow Conjurer cocked his head and looked at Alex with pity. His finger flicked the air. The Rag-O-Roc behind Alex wrapped him in a crushing embrace.

"Of course they didn't tell you anything. I never thought they had. You are merely bait to lure your parents out of hiding."

EMMA

The fog tickled the hairs standing straight up on Emma's arms. She gripped the paddle tight, ready to swing, and glanced back at Pimawa, thankful she was not alone.

The looming shadows in the fog slipped closer to the canoe, where the two of them sat waiting.

"Ahoy!" called a voice out of the wall of gray.

"You heard that, right?" Emma asked Pimawa.

"I did," Pimawa agreed. "I'm sure you would know better than I, but I don't believe Rag-O-Rocs can speak."

Emma and Pimawa watched in awe as a fleet of boats drifted out of the fog. In the lead was a small skiff. Rofflo and Jukstra crouched at the bow, leaning on their oars. Behind them, Royan adjusted the rudder to avoid the canoe.

"Ahoy!" said Jukstra. "Quite a challenge, trying to find you in this murk."

Relief turned to anger as Emma frowned at the three Jimjarians. "You can turn your search party around. Go tell Derren we're not coming back."

"That's good to hear," said Derren Fallow. He and Rowlfin drifted alongside the other two boats in a wide dory. "I'd have to tell everyone they came a long way for nothing."

Boat after boat appeared, filled with Jimjarians and Conjurians. Emma watched, stunned. She lost count at twenty vessels, with still more too far back in the mist to see. "What are all of you doing here?"

"It would seem that some young man spread the story of a certain girl who took on three Rag-O-Rocs and won. And who was willing to stand up to the Shadow Conjurer." Derren ran his fingers through his damp hair and scratched the back of his head. "As you can see, that gave a lot of people hope. Including me." Derren laughed. "Besides, I had no one left to run away with."

Emma scanned the boats. "Alex? Is he . . . ?"

"I'm sorry, Emma," said Derren. "We couldn't find your brother. Or Savachia, either."

Emma nodded, trying not to let the hurt show. She hadn't really expected to see her brother. Alex was off on his own quest. Emma could only hope he would succeed.

But Savachia? After he'd agreed to help her? After he'd made that speech? It was funny how the boy kept convincing her to trust him. To believe in him.

But she had to admit to herself that he'd kept his end of the bargain. She had her army. She swore, if she survived, she would fulfill her end of the deal. If Alex really did have the Eye of Dedi, Emma would have to find some way of getting it to Savachia.

That was for later, though. Now she had a job to do.

Slowly she got to her feet. Her legs wobbled. Hopefully they all thought it was the canoe's fault.

She felt as if the fog had seeped into her head. All these people here because of her! It was what she had wanted, wasn't it? Shouldn't she say something? Not a single word came to mind. A gentle paw pressed against her back.

"Miss E—I mean, Emma," said Pimawa. "Are you all right?"

Her mind cleared. Despite her nerves and the sensation that her throat was closing, she realized she'd already said everything she needed to. Or, rather, Savachia had said it for her.

These people weren't here because of her words. They were looking at her now, bobbing in the open water, because of her actions.

"Yes. Yes, I am," she answered. She sat, turned the canoe around, and paddled. Pimawa followed her lead.

CHAPTER 14

SAVACHIA

In a cavern below Conjurian City, Gertie sat patiently on a narrow, pebbly beach, her legs folded underneath her, steam hissing out of her wet joints. She cranked her mechanical head around to investigate the thumping noise that was coming from the rear of the carriage.

A panel underneath a puppet theater mounted on the rear of the carriage buckled outward. The thumping came again and again until the bolts holding the panel popped loose. Savachia's crumpled body tumbled out.

Moaning, he stretched his legs, rubbing them vigorously. He pulled himself up. Then he lumbered forward, patting Gertie on the head as he gazed off into the tunnel.

"Guess I don't need to ask which way they went," Savachia muttered.

EMMA

As Emma paddled toward the shore, fear and resolve were battling it out in her cramped chest. The landscape ahead was spookily quiet. A thin sheet of dust mixed with the fog blanketing the shore.

Emma and Pimawa, reaching land first, disembarked without a word. The other boats scraped up onto the rocky beach. Soon the shoreline was full of humans and Jimjarians, frozen in shock at the destruction laid out before them.

Through the dense gray fog, they spotted glimpses of what had once been the greatest city in the Conjurian. It seemed that once the Rag-O-Rocs had finished with the Tower of Dedi, they'd started in on the other buildings. Through the fog, Emma could see roofs with gaping holes, streets with torn-up cobblestones, houses that leaned perilously toward their neighbors.

Everyone on the beach was looking at Emma. At the moment, her fear was pummeling the snot out of her resolve.

"What's the plan?" whispered Derren as he came up behind Emma. "Do we have one? Or should we set up the volleyball nets?"

Pimawa scowled at him.

"Hey." Derren held his hands up. "Just trying to ease the tension."

What had Emma brought these people into? Why had she thought she could lead an army? But someone had to do something. The first step was obvious. She'd think about the next step later.

"Let's get everyone off the beach," said Emma. Her legs felt hollow, but she moved forward. "Head toward that old warehouse for cover."

Derren and Pimawa spread the word to the troops. Everyone followed Emma into the old brick building. From inside, through the gaps in the roof, they could all see the occasional form of a Rag-O-Roc swooping through the fog. But the flying skeletons did not seem to have noticed the rag-tag invading army.

"How far are we from the Tower?" she asked Pimawa in a low voice.

"About five blocks that way," Pimawa answered. "The streets between us and the Tower are narrow. With luck, we should escape detection from above until we reach the field where the Tower stands. Where it stood, I should say. And then . . ."

And then indeed, Emma thought. She knew that charging straight for the Tower would be sure death. Right now they had the element of surprise. Once they hit the open field, they'd be exposed. The Rag-O-Rocs would pick them off easily.

What they needed was a distraction.

"These warehouses—are they empty?" asked Emma.

"I'm not sure," said Pimawa. "Most of them belonged to illusion manufacturers. Sales dried up years ago. I would imagine there are a few odds and ends collecting dust."

It was Emma's turn to smile at Derren. "You're up. You were—what did you call it? A methodologist? You created magic tricks for my parents' stage show?"

"That's right." Derren frowned as if he didn't quite follow her.

Emma gestured toward the interior of the warehouse. "Take as many people as you need into this warehouse and the ones nearby. We're going to need misdirection."

"Ah." Derren smiled.

"I can go," Pimawa offered.

"Derren's got this." Emma held Pimawa back.

"Yes, I do. It's about time I put my skills to use once more." Derren jogged off to round up his team, then turned back to Emma. "It feels good to be scrounging up tricks for a Maskelyne again."

ALEX

Still firmly held by the Rag-O-Roc behind him, Alex gaped at the Shadow Conjurer. "What do you mean, lure my parents out of hiding?" he asked. "They're dead. My parents are dead."

"I will show you why this world is not worth saving. I will show you what your parents could not see," the Shadow Conjurer said as if he hadn't heard Alex's words. He clapped his hands three times.

Another Rag-O-Roc soared up onto the platform, carrying a limp figure. It dumped the moaning body at its master's feet: a girl not much older than Emma, her face still covered by a black veil.

Tenyo.

Alex had seen her only two days before this. She was a mentalist—or she'd claimed to be. She was supposed to try to read Alex's mind for clues about where the Eye might be. But she'd had no real magical power. She'd been a fraud.

That didn't mean she deserved this.

"All the pitiful souls like this one were empty husks before I tried squeezing out what droplets of magic remained in them." The Shadow Conjurer lifted Tenyo with both hands. She hung limply from his grasp. "Consider this an opening act, if you will. And a preview of your future."

Blue light flowed from the copper pedestal into the ring in the Shadow Conjurer's chest. From there, it sparked down his arms into Tenyo. "She was one of the last to have actual magical powers—ah, you didn't know that? Yes, she was indeed powerful. For a time. But then her powers, like so many others', faded to nothing. She resorted to trickery. At least now she can serve some purpose."

Tenyo was completely engulfed in blue light. The Shadow Conjurer dropped her twitching body. Before Alex's horrified gaze, Tenyo bent and twisted. Her limbs shriveled. Her

torso shrank. In moments, nothing but a skeleton was left, with a black veil that still clung to the Rag-O-Roc's face as it shrieked.

Alex wrestled against the Rag-O-Roc holding him. The creature hissed in his ear, tightening its grip.

"Once your parents learn I have you," the Shadow Conjurer went on, reaching out with his arms toward Alex, "they will come running with the Eye. They will want to trade it for your safety. Of course, there isn't any possibility that you will be safe—but they won't know that, will they?"

Alex knew his time was running out. What had just happened to Tenyo was about to happen to him—unless he could figure out what to do with the Eye.

Alex bit down on the Rag-O-Roc's finger and shook his head violently. The finger snapped off. The creature hissed in displeasure but did not loosen its grip.

Alex spat the fragment of bone at the Shadow Conjurer.

"So what if you *do* get your hands on the Eye? Do you even know how to use it?" he challenged.

The Shadow Conjurer paused. His red scars crinkled. Alex had found a sore spot.

"Tell me then, oh great and maniacal moron, how does the Eye work?" said Alex. "You have all this cool-looking equipment, but I don't think you built it. Someone else did. Someone smarter than you."

The veins in the Shadow Conjurer's neck bulged. His hands clenched. Then his grayish lips pulled back into a crazed smile.

"You will never know," he whispered. He lunged for Alex, seizing his arms, ripping him from the Rag-O-Roc's grip.

The Shadow Conjurer's stolen power seared into Alex. His jaw locked shut, preventing him from screaming.

He'd misplayed his hand. He hadn't lured the Shadow Conjurer into telling him what he needed to know—he'd just made the guy mad.

Mad enough to do to Alex what he'd just done to Tenyo?

But then the Shadow Conjurer froze. Suddenly he flung Alex to the ground. He was watching his minions above, who were screeching loudly as they swarmed away from what was left of the Tower.

"What's this?" said the Shadow Conjurer. "Someone has decided to fight back?" His laughter echoed. "If people had cared this much a hundred years ago, I might never have been needed."

As Alex lay on his back twitching, he knew who would be leading the charge. She had done it. His sister had taken the battle to the Shadow Conjurer, and she had raised an army to do it. He felt a proud smile on his face, but it quickly faded.

Emma had no idea what she was rushing into. His sister didn't stand a chance. But Alex's plan could still work—if only he could move.

CHAPTER 15

EMMA

Black roots arched out of the ground. Jagged bits of debris poked up through the fog that clung around the remains of the Tower of Dedi. Although the fog lay low to the ground, there was enough of it for the five Myst fish that charged across the open space.

Emma clung to the lead fish, with Pimawa and the three young Jimjarians behind in an arrow formation. The distance had seemed a lot shorter from the safety of the surrounding warehouses.

"Keep up!" Rofflo yelled back at Royan and Jukstra.

"We're hurrying, we're hurrying. Calm your whiskers," huffed Jukstra.

"Emma!" Pimawa pointed up at the sky. "Here they come!"

Emma didn't look up. She kept her eyes on the giant tree stump ahead, with the scrap of stone wall still clinging to it.

The Rag-O-Rocs spiraled down in front of the steps that led up to the remains of the Tower's entrance. Then they changed course, flying in a tight formation straight at Emma and the four Jimjarians.

Seconds before the first Rag-O-Roc would collide with her, Emma yelled, "Now!"

Derren and his team of about sixty Jimjarians and Conjurians popped up from behind nearby roots. They hoisted large, brightly painted tubes over their heads.

Derren had told Emma that this was an illusion first designed by her uncle Mordo. The "Tele-porto" was what he had called it. He would transport audience members from one side of the theater to the other.

Now Rag-O-Rocs, unable to change course in time, swooped into the tubes and vanished.

The Rag-O-Rocs behind them, confused, broke in the opposite direction to avoid the trap. Before they could regroup, Rowlfin and the second wave of Emma's army popped up at the edges of the field, whooping and hollering, sprinting across the field, further distracting the Rag-O-Rocs.

Enraged, the creatures darted every which way after the chaotic masses.

The Jimjarians and Conjurians who were now being pursued by Rag-O-Rocs ran for their lives, diving into a series of brightly colored boxes that had been set up along the perimeter of the field. Their pursuers followed their prey into the boxes. The sides of the boxes fell away, revealing cages with steel bars. Inside the cages, Rag-O-Rocs gnashed their teeth and gripped the bars as if to throttle them.

Jimjarians and Conjurians crawled out from underneath the cages, cheering and exchanging hugs and high fives.

"We didn't get them all!" shouted Rowlfin, pointing toward the tree.

The cheering died.

The few remaining Rag-O-Rocs had peeled off at the last second, returning to hunt their original targets.

"Almost there!" Emma shouted. She focused on the steps, only twenty yards away, that led up to the Tower's old entrance. And then she caught a flash of bone and tattered cloth in her peripheral vision.

They weren't going to make it. A Rag-O-Roc came in

fast on her right. Before it could snatch her up, Pimawa's fish swooped in, sideswiping the creature. The Rag-O-Roc smashed into Pimawa, and they rolled off in a white blur of bone and fur.

"Pimawa!" Emma cried out. She tried turning her fish around but with no success. Alarmed by the ambush, her fish went full speed toward the tree.

She twisted her head around to see Pimawa rolling across the ground, grappling with the Rag-O-Roc. He had his arms wrapped tightly around the creature's spine and was holding on with all his might. It freed its skeletal arms and raised them like spears.

Emma gasped. Was she about to lose Pimawa just as she'd lost Uncle Mordo? And her parents, so long ago?

Then she saw Rowlfin dive off his own Myst fish and crash into the Rag-O-Roc, flattening it onto the dirt.

"Get moving!" yelled Rowlfin as the Rag-O-Roc bucked wildly. "Emma needs you!"

Shaking with relief, Emma flung herself off her fish right next to the scarred stump that had once been the Tower of Dedi. She slung a bag off her shoulders and unpacked the contents: a thick rope and four wooden spools, each about as long as her forearm.

Pimawa, now released from the Rag-O-Roc's clutches, bounded across the room and landed beside her, flanked by Rofflo, Royan, and Jukstra.

Emma beamed at Pimawa, who smiled briefly back. "Are you ready?" she asked.

"What do you think is waiting for us in there?" said Royan nervously.

"Hopefully a buffet," said Jukstra.

"Focus, boys," said Pimawa. "Emma, are *you* ready?"

Emma nodded, handing each of them a spool.

"Master Mordo always said this stuff was impossible to master," Pimawa commented as he glanced at the label on top of the spool. It read ULTRA-VECTRA INVISIBLE THREAD. "I hope he was exaggerating."

Emma stood, hoisting the rope onto her shoulder, wincing at the weight on her wound. "Okay, you guys know what to do. I'm sure you'll succeed. But if I don't . . . make it, you get out of there, understand?" She didn't want to drag this out, afraid she'd lose her nerve. "Let's go."

The four Jimjarians nodded and headed for the stairs that led to what remained of the entrance to the Tower.

Emma felt in her belt to be sure the pick given to her by her parents was still there, then headed around the stump until she was at the side opposite the entrance. She reached up, grabbed the jagged bark, and began to climb.

ALEX

Alex heard some sort of commotion coming from the entrance to the Tower. He tried to roll over onto his side to watch, but he could not get his body to move. It was as if the magical energy that had poured out of the Shadow Conjurer and into his body had paralyzed him.

With a painful effort, he dragged his head to one side. He saw the Tower doors scrape open, hanging awkwardly on their bent hinges.

Pimawa rushed in first, then skidded to a halt. Pimawa? What was Pimawa doing here? Royan, Jukstra, and Rofflo were behind him. They all stopped too, the same stunned expression stretching over their furry faces.

Their voices drifted faintly to Alex's ears. "Is that Rag-O-Roc wearing a veil?" asked Jukstra.

"Well, what do you know," mumbled Royan. "You *can* make them more terrifying."

"Steady, boys." Pimawa crouched, holding up his spool. "Let's do what we came to do."

As Alex stared, Royan, Jukstra, and Rofflo held their spools with both hands. They ran and leaped precariously around the perimeter of the old stump, landing on one bit of broken floor after another. Each held a big wooden spool high in his paws and sometimes jumped to swipe or swing that spool at a jutting piece of bark.

Was this what it looked like when Jimjarians lost their minds?

The Shadow Conjurer watched with a look of mild curiosity. He grinned down at Alex. "That is certainly the worst rescue attempt in history," he said. He snapped his fingers. "Fetch them."

The Rag-O-Roc that had once been Tenyo took off, flying straight at Pimawa.

"Hold tight, boys!" yelled Pimawa.

The veiled Rag-O-Roc shrieked. Pimawa tensed, holding his ground. A loud twanging noise echoed around the tree walls. The Rag-O-Roc, claws extended, hung inches from Pimawa's face, struggling against something invisible.

"How long will it hold?" shouted Jukstra.

"Hopefully long enough," Pimawa called back.

A faint slithering noise caught Alex's attention. Painfully, he turned his head the other way and saw a rope drop down from the ruined wall opposite the entrance. One end now dangled over the platform where he lay.

Behind the Shadow Conjurer's back, Emma climbed over the wall and slid down the rope.

Alex tried to warn her, but he couldn't unclench his jaw. All the Shadow Conjurer would have to do was turn around, and he could see Alex's crazy sister in her pink leggings, climbing straight into danger.

She landed behind the gateway, gesturing for Alex to stay quiet. As if he had a choice. Her eyes narrowed, locked onto the Shadow Conjurer's back. Alex had never seen her this angry or this focused. Not even after the time he had filled her pillow with flour.

Emma came out from her hiding place with her pick held high. Lying helpless, Alex watched his sister strike the Shadow Conjurer at full speed. She went right through him and hit the platform wrapped up in an empty robe.

"Trying to surprise a magician?" the Shadow Conjurer said, strolling out from the shadows. "Rather a doomed effort."

Emma threw off the robe and charged again. The Shadow Conjurer's arm shot forward, and his hand grabbed her throat.

Alex felt his muscles beginning to relax. Too late to do any real good. "Let her go!" he croaked, looking at his sister struggling in the Shadow Conjurer's grip. "You should never have come. I had a plan," he told her.

"This was your plan? Getting caught?" Emma gurgled. She yanked at the Shadow Conjurer's wrist.

Alex rolled over and forced himself

to his hands and knees. All his muscles felt stiff and soggy at once. But he had to move. Had to help Emma. Had to . . .

EMMA

Emma couldn't breathe. Her throat, with the Shadow Conjurer's hand clenched around it, hurt like nothing ever had.

She kicked and flailed, but it was no use. She couldn't free herself. Couldn't kill him. Couldn't save Alex. Couldn't even save herself.

Over the Shadow Conjurer's shoulder, she glimpsed Pimawa ducking under a trapped Rag-O-Roc with a veiled face and heading toward her on the narrow bridge. She saw Derren rushing in through the doorway, Jimjarians and Conjurians at his back.

But a Rag-O-Roc plunged down from above and smashed through the narrow passageway that led to the platform where she, Alex, and the Shadow Conjurer were stranded. Derren and his troops skidded to a halt while Pimawa staggered, lost his balance, and fell.

Pimawa managed to grab with both paws at the edge of the platform. But how long could he hold on?

How long could Emma herself hold on?

Her plan was a failure. Her attack had fizzled. All she could think of was one thing—the Shadow Conjurer must not get his hands on the Eye of Dedi. No matter what.

"Alex, don't give it to him!" she choked out.

The Shadow Conjurer's eyeless face looked puzzled for a moment. Then his head snapped around, and he sneered at Alex. "You found it, didn't you? You clever, clever young man." He turned back to Emma and grinned. "Amateurs are horrible at keeping secrets."

Emma saw despair fall over Alex's face. "He didn't know I had it, Emma," her brother said. He sat up painfully, but he didn't seem to have the strength to do anything else. "He just wanted me as bait to lure Mom and Dad out of hiding. I think—I think maybe—they're not dead."

"They will be soon," said the Shadow Conjurer. "Once they come looking for you." He lowered Emma to the ground and shifted his grip to the front of her T-shirt. "Both of you."

Burning with rage, Emma raked her free hand across the Shadow Conjurer's face. His skin caught in her fingernails. She wrenched her hand back, taking the Shadow Conjurer's face with her.

A flimsy mask dangled from Emma's fingers, and she stared into Angel Xavier's face.

Angel Xavier?

Angel Xavier, who had walked through walls and escaped from locked cages and caught bullets in his teeth while Emma watched, breathless? Angel Xavier, who'd vanished from the Conjurian just as Emma and Alex had arrived?

"You—you—" stammered Emma. She flung the mask to the floor in horror. "You faked your disappearance?"

"Misdirection," said Angel with a chuckle. "If every magician believed the Shadow Conjurer had abducted Angel Xavier, then Angel Xavier couldn't possibly *be* the Shadow Conjurer. Your parents know all about faking death."

Emma shook her head, hardly knowing what she was protesting.

"Your parents used my own 'buried alive' illusion to convince the world that they were dead and that the Eye was lost forever. But in truth they gave the Eye to your little brother? How charming."

Angel tightened his grip on Emma's shirt and shifted his gaze to Alex.

"Your parents wanted to learn about it, study it." He sounded disgusted. "I want to use it to save our world. To save magic. Magicians should rule the world—*both* worlds! I want to show the Flatworld *true* magic. And now I will."

"Hey," said Alex. "Let her go and I'll give you the Eye."

"Alex! Don't!" Emma shouted. She clawed at Angel Xavier's hand with both of hers. He hardly seemed to notice.

"I know what I'm doing," Alex told her. He got shakily to his feet, put a hand into his pocket, and pulled it out with a small pebble resting on it. "I said, let her go and you can have this."

A cruel smile widened on Angel's face. "I will have the Eye whether or not I let your sister go," he told Alex. "The only question is, how painful will her end be? Give me the Eye now and I will make it quick. If not—"

Snowflakes fluttered past the Shadow Conjurer's scarred face. The flakes intensified into a swirling snowstorm. Suddenly Emma couldn't see anything but herself, her brother, the Shadow Conjurer, and a whirling whiteness.

"What is this?" said the Shadow Conjurer. "More pathetic tricks?"

A frantic clomping noise grew louder and closer. As the snowstorm swirled away into a light squall, Gertie leaped through the entrance to the Tower. Derren had just pulled Pimawa to safety, and Gertie vaulted over their heads, soaring over the gap in the passageway and landing in the middle of the platform.

Savachia was clutching her neck. With a wild grin, he looked down at the Eye resting on Alex's palm.

"You might want to put that somewhere safe," he said. Then he rolled off Gertie and toward Angel Xavier. "Both of you. Get out of here!" Savachia shouted.

Angel Xavier turned away, covering his bleeding face. Emma struggled to her feet, breathless, gasping, and smiling. Savachia had not run away. He hadn't let her down. He was here. He was leaping at the Shadow Conjurer with a fist pulled back, ready for the final blow.

Angel spun around, catching Savachia with a ferocious roundhouse punch. Savachia thudded to the ground, out cold.

"Em, let's go!" yelled Alex, scrambling toward Gertie.

Emma staggered to her feet, grabbing the fallen pick. She raised it and swung.

Angel Xavier dodged the swing. His hand clamped around Emma's throat for the second time. A two of diamonds protruded from his forehead. Blue light sparked from his vest. "Give me the Eye now!" he snarled.

ALEX

Alex knew there was no way he could let this creep murder his sister. "Okay, okay!" He moved as close to Angel as he dared and stretched out his hand holding the plain gray pebble with the dark band around it. "Just don't hurt her!"

With the hand that was not strangling Emma, Angel gingerly lifted the Eye from Alex's palm.

"A magician without true power is nothing more than a con man." Angel's voice was oddly soothing. "He will fool you into giving him your money willingly. A magician with real power—now that is someone who doesn't have to fool you. That is a god.

"Once I unlock the Eye, a new age will dawn for magic!" he went on. "But I would hate to waste the little that is left of the power I have drained from this dead world. I shall give it to your sister. A parting gift."

Flickers of blue light ran from Angel Xavier's chest, up through his arm, and into Emma. She stiffened, teeth gritted, eyes wider than humanly possible. Angel Xavier released her. She fell like a board.

CHAPTER 16

ALEX

The newly created Rag-O-Roc was still a bit wobbly. Alex stared at the blue pajama shirt wrapped around its exposed ribs. The creature pulled itself toward him. Alex retreated and tripped, falling onto the platform. Behind the approaching monstrosity that used to be his sister, he saw Angel Xavier place the Eye into his chest plate.

"Emma, I'm so sorry," Alex whispered helplessly. "I'm sorry."

The Rag-O-Roc lashed out, piercing Alex's shoe and the foot inside it with a bony finger. The stabbing pain shook Alex back into life. He yanked his foot loose from its shoe and kicked the Rag-O-Roc in the head.

It fell backward, confused and hissing, shaking its skull.

Alex hobbled over to Savachia and shook the boy as hard as he could. "C'mon. Let's go. We have to get away from here!" But Savachia didn't stir.

Alex yanked the boy's limp body toward the edge of the platform. But he could only move it a foot at a time, and the Rag-O-Roc that had been Emma was getting to its feet.

Suddenly Savachia's body jerked straight up into the air. Gertie had his shirt clamped in her mouth. She hoisted the boy onto her back. Then the metal alpaca knelt. Alex flung himself onto Gertie and clasped both arms around her neck. "Run!" he told her.

The alpaca clopped her metal hoof on the ledge. But she didn't move.

The Rag-O-Roc in the pajama shirt lurched forward. Behind it, Angel Xavier spread his arms wide. The Eye sparkled orange in his chest. Angel threw his head back with a hideous smile. "The time for magic to rule is now!"

A loud hissing sound came from the Eye. Perplexed, Angel looked down at his chest. The Eye sizzled.

"What?" Angel tugged at the Eye. It was clamped firmly in place. He ripped off his gloves, fumbling for the Eye with his bare fingers. Sparks seared his skin, and he snatched his hand away. He glared at Alex. "What did you do?"

"Gertie, go!" Alex kicked his heels, desperately trying to get the alpaca to jump. Gertie shook her head and stepped away from the edge of the platform. Could this mechanical contraption made of metal and magic actually be afraid of heights?

The Rag-O-Roc lurched forward and raked its claws

across Gertie's flank. The shock seemed to scare Gertie into action. Her back legs bent and leaped off the platform, just at the instant that Angel Xavier erupted in a blinding explosion.

Gertie plunged down, skidding along the stalagmite that supported the platform, her metal hooves smashing glass tubes as she went. Halfway down, Alex flew off. End over end he tumbled until he smashed to a stop at the bottom, against a glass cylinder.

Rocks and dirt rained down. Above, smoke twisted into a cloudy bouquet of sickly purple and orange flames. The smell of charred wood burned Alex's eyes and throat.

"Alex!"

The voice was muffled, barely audible in Alex's ringing ears. Alex blinked. When he opened his eyes, Neil and Clive stood over him.

"Well, googly-moogly, my boy," said Neil. "That went all wibbly-wobbly. There was your sister's all-out attack, and then that street urchin almost ran Clive and me over with our own alpaca. Goodness."

Alex stared up at Neil, limp with despair. He was tired . . . and he hurt . . . and his sister was gone.

"Let's get you back to the carriage," said Neil. "Clive! We need to track down the rest of Gertie, and I suppose we should find that urchin, Savachia, too. Hup, hup, my boy!" He extended a hand to Alex. "Let's not sit around like a Rag-O-Roc buffet."

Alex ignored Neil's hand and lay back on the cold ground. Emma was a Rag-O-Roc now. He hadn't been able to save her.

The smoke parted, and Neil darted back as a dark shadow with a shoe hanging from its claw plunged toward Alex.

Without thinking, Alex rolled to his left, just missing the Rag-O-Roc's sharp fingers. He kept rolling until he was under one of the cylinders. Hissing, the Rag-O-Roc jammed its long arm under the cylinder, trying to pull him out. Alex shimmied out the other side, but the enraged creature had hooked his sweatshirt.

Alex raised his arms, allowing the sweatshirt to slip off. He crawled through, under, and around the maze of tubes, hoping he could find the tunnel that led out of this nightmare.

Two long arms reached out from the other side of a cylinder and grabbed him, dragging him behind the glass tube. Alex almost shouted with alarm, but then he saw that it was Clive who held him, not a Rag-O-Roc.

Clive released him, holding a finger to his lips. Alex nodded. He'd be quiet. He'd hold still. And maybe the Rag-O-Roc that had been his sister would not find them here.

Or maybe she would.

Like a shadow leaping across a wall when a light is

switched on, the Rag-O-Roc sprang up behind Clive, seizing him and tossing the tall man into the cave wall.

Then the monster bounded at Alex, knocking him down and crushing him against the ground. Black spots crept along the edges of Alex's vision.

"Emma." Alex could hardly hear his own voice. "Please, Emma, if it's still you—"

The creature snarled. Alex's ribs creaked as air wheezed from his chest.

"Alex! Catch!" Neil emerged from the smoke. He tossed something small and light toward Alex.

Through watery eyes, Alex glimpsed what was flying at him—a tiny gray pebble. He reached up to catch it, and it bounced off his palm and onto the cave floor.

The Rag-O-Roc's skull came down closer and closer. Alex stretched his arm till his shoulder flared with pain. His fingers curled around the tiny rock.

He was suffocating. He estimated another ten seconds before he blacked out. He squeezed the Eye of Dedi.

Belief was a funny thing indeed. If he wanted to know how far back to pull his slingshot to hit his sister with a water balloon from twenty feet away, he could do the math and hit her every time. No belief needed. When he'd wanted to give his mechanical dog, Bartleby, the ability to wiggle his ears, he'd needed only to design the right configuration of gears and springs.

No amount of research or math would save Emma—or Alex himself. But in his mind, past all the stored equations and engineering principles and laws of physics, burned a spark the size of a molecule. Something told him that spark was his only hope now. Barely smoldering, it required no advanced math, no evidence, no schematics. It only needed Alex to believe.

Alex focused on that spark. It flickered out. No! He would not let it go. He'd burn every scrap of knowledge in his brain if that was what it took. He tossed it all into the fire: periodic tables, migration patterns of the Jurassic period, *The Complete Works of Sir Francis Bacon*. All of it. The spark roared. Flames engulfed his mind.

A soothing warmth spread up his arm. His hand glowed, the same way it would if he held it over a flashlight. Rays of orange spiked out from between his closed fingers, so bright he clamped his eyes shut. The insides of his eyelids burned as if the sun were hovering inches away.

All around he heard what sounded like sacks of bones hitting the ground. He was floating, or at least it felt as if he were. All the pain melted away.

The light vanished. Alex opened his eyes, expecting to see something wondrous. Instead, he saw a Rag-O-Roc's skull resting on his chest. Its bony fingers still clenched his shirt, but whatever life it had had, if you could call it that, was gone.

Alex turned his head. A few feet away, another Rag-O-Roc lay in an awkward pile of bones. At first he thought his tears were distorting the shape of the bones. But it was actually changing before his eyes.

Slowly, the pile of bones fleshed out into arms, legs, and a head. He didn't recognize the face. A man with enormous sideburns and a bulbous nose lay where the Rag-O-Roc had been. The man sputtered. Drool rolled down his double chin. His eyes flickered under the lids, then opened. Moaning, the man turned onto his side, looking straight at Alex.

"You're alive?" said Alex.

Alex turned his head back the other way. His sister lay across him, tattered pajama shirt and all.

The smoke cleared. All around, people who had once been Rag-O-Rocs stood up, woozy, dizzy, confused. Others lay on the ground, unconscious still.

"My boy! My boy!" Neil struggled to climb over the glass chamber in front of Alex. "Show of the century! Those things fell out of the sky. They're all changing back! It's the greatest magic I've ever seen! That anyone's ever seen! How did you do it?"

"I have no idea," said Alex. He put his arms around Emma.

Her eyes fluttered open. She tried raising her head, wincing in pain.

"Take it easy, Em," said Alex. "You did it. We did it. We beat the Shadow Conjurer. Angel Xavier. Remember?"

"How?" She blinked, and her mouth opened as her memory streamed back. "You gave him the Eye!"

"I switched it," said Alex. "I switched it with a woofle seed."

"He had a bit of help, I might add." Neil fumbled in his pocket. He whipped out a card and proudly displayed it to Emma.

"The two of clubs?" asked Emma.

"Huh? What? No." Neil shook the card. It changed into an accordion photo holder, cascading a series of pictures of Neil and several cats wearing a variety of costumes. "Heh, never mind those." He shook the photos, snapped them up into his hand, and transformed them into a copper badge embossed with the MAGE logo.

"You're agents?" asked Emma. "Like our parents?"

"Undercover agents," added Alex. "They told me after they kidnapped me."

"I prefer to think of it as rescuing you," Neil said.

"We worked out this plan together," Alex went on, ignoring Neil. "They'd hand me over to the Shadow Conjurer, and I'd get him to tell me how the Eye worked. Then I'd give him the woofle seed. Neil was keeping the Eye safe for me all along."

"Yes indeed." Neil tried to look modest and failed. "No need to glorify our endeavors. They are truly spectacular on their own. When rumors of this Shadow Conjurer first emerged, Master Agglar assigned us to investigate. You know, the usual risk-your-life-among-the-dregs-of-society type job. Dig around and find out exactly what this phantom was planning." Neil plopped down, cross-legged.

"Our first lead was a bounty placed on two children. The Maskelyne children. If we could find you, we figured that we'd have a chance to get close to whoever was paying that bounty. However, the Shadow Conjurer beat us to the punch. Somehow he knew Mordo was hiding you both."

With a grimace, Emma propped up on her elbow. "And the Shadow—I mean Angel Xavier—is he . . . ?"

Neil separated his clasped hands, wiggling his fingers, miming an explosion. "The great and powerful Angel Xavier went boom-boom. Still looks a bit smoldery up there right now. I daresay he survived it and hightailed it through the gateway. I certainly would, in his circumstances."

"What about them?" Alex pointed around at the cylinders.

Neil craned his neck, his eyes circling around the vast number of cylinders, each with a person still inside. "One miracle at a time, my boy."

"Was it a dream, or did you pitch me off a cliff?" Savachia hobbled into view, leaning on Clive. Or possibly the other way around. Seeing Emma, Savachia limped as quickly as he could to her side. "Is she okay?"

Neil patted him on the back. "That is the zillion-dollar question. And this is not the time nor the place for a quiz show."

"Thanks." Alex smiled at Savachia. "Pretty dramatic rescue attempt. Not bad for a con man."

"Sure," said Savachia, rubbing his face gingerly. "Anytime you need me to get clobbered by a psycho trying to destroy the world, just call."

"We're coming! Hang on!" Pimawa's voice rang down into the cavern.

"We'll be here," Alex shouted back, regretting it instantly, as the effort of yelling made stabbing pains ricochet around his chest and down through one leg.

Alex had risked everything for answers. Now he only had more questions. But he also had Emma back. Right now, that was enough.

CHAPTER 17

ALEX

Alex took his time crossing the field over to the Tree of Dedi. His left leg still ached from his tumble down into the cavern underneath the gateway, and he had to lean on a cane to walk.

The wind picked up, blowing in a smell of the sea, mixed with one of charred wood. All around, crews worked tirelessly, removing the last of the debris from the fallen Tower.

It had been a week since they'd defeated the Shadow Conjurer, also known as Angel Xavier. Since then, Jimjarians and magicians had worked around the clock, helping the recovering Rag-O-Rocs and freeing the captives in the Shadow Conjurer's cylinders.

Reaching the steps of the Tower, Alex took a breath,

looking up at the system of pulleys lining the top of the crumbling wall. He had helped design the array of specialized cranes while confined to his hospital bed. Leaning back against a large root, he watched as another glass-and-copper cylinder was hoisted out carefully and lowered to the ground. How many were left?

Slowly, Alex climbed the steps. Most of the people who had been changed back from Rag-O-Rocs were up and about. Even Emma had recovered more quickly than Alex. Those imprisoned in the glass chambers hadn't fared as well. Most had survived, but they were weak and shaken, their magical powers depleted—perhaps for good.

Try as he might, Alex had not been able to activate the Eye again. Not even a spark. Now, squeezing the small object in his pocket, he could almost believe it was nothing more than an ordinary pebble. He could not, however, deny the "occurrence" (as he liked to call it) that had returned his sister to him.

From the old Tower entrance, Alex watched Derren Fallow, surrounded by Jimjarians wearing hard hats, direct the rescue effort. Another canister rose from the cavern below.

"Stop! Swing it out another three feet," Derren yelled to Royan and Jukstra, who were operating the crane on the far side of the tree. "Nice and steady. Good! You're clear. Bring it up!"

Royan and Jukstra cranked a winch. Inch by inch, the cylinder rose.

Rofflo stood next to Derren, making notes on a clipboard. He showed what he had written to Derren, who sighed, took off his hard hat, and wiped his brow.

"We'll get there," said Derren. "We'll get them all out." He did a double take when he noticed Alex behind him. "Hey! Clean bill of health? Or did Pimawa kidnap you through some secret tunnel?"

Alex regarded the man he'd once dreamed of running away to. Back then, he'd thought that Derren would rescue him from all the difficulties of life with his uncle. He had since learned that Derren Fallow wasn't perfect. Then again, who was?

Alex held out the Eye.

Derren's arm stayed at his side. "Are you sure? You might need it on your trip."

Alex lifted his hand higher. "It needs to be kept safe until I learn how it works. And I will. I promise."

Taking the Eye, Derren furrowed one eyebrow. "You trust me? I mean, I didn't turn out to be the savior you thought I was."

"A lot of people weren't what I thought they were," said Alex. "Besides, you're in charge of the city now."

"Temporarily." Derren pinched the bridge of his nose, the fatigue showing on his face. "And not by choice. It seems I was the only one who didn't nominate me for the job."

"That's because you've always been there for them," said Alex. "You were there for me and Em when it counted."

They both remained silent, watching Rofflo yank on his ears as one of the glass tubes bounced off the side of the tree.

"Hey, you two!" Rofflo shouted at the other young Jimjarians. "Try it with your eyes open."

"Any sign of him?" asked Alex, focusing on the scorched platform where only a few charred bits of the gateway remained.

"Angel Xavier?" said Derren. "No, nothing. The gateway was badly damaged. Who knows when or if we'll get it working again. The Eye might help . . . if only we can figure out how to use it."

Alex shuffled his feet.

"Hey," said Derren. "No one's blaming you for not knowing how you did what you did. You're a hero, Alex."

"What if Angel Xavier escaped through the gateway?" asked Alex. "What if he comes back through one of the illegal gates? Like the one we came through?"

With a comforting wink, Derren clapped his hand on Alex's shoulder. "That is the Grubians' first assignment as the new heads of MAGE: to secure all unauthorized gateways. If he survived, I will find him," Derren went on, more serious now. "I promise." Derren held up the Eye. "I guess you and I were both wrong about this little rock, huh? Made believers out of both of us."

"I think so," said Alex. "There aren't always answers. Sometimes all you have is belief."

"Well, I believe that, with enough time, we will learn more about the Eye. And we will find a way to revive magic." Derren squeezed Alex's shoulder. "You and Emma will. I'm sure of it."

Alex blushed. "I should get back to her. We have to get going."

"Are you sure you're up for it?"

"Doesn't matter," said Alex. "It's what we have to do."

Alex stepped back, flushed, wondering what to say next. Derren made it easy for him.

"No goodbyes." Derren tossed the Eye up and caught it, clenching his fingers tight. "I will guard this with my life until you return."

Alex was spared any further awkwardness when Rofflo shouted colorful phrases at Royan and Jukstra.

"Till then, Master Maskelyne!" Derren slapped his hard hat on and turned back to Rofflo, who seemed on the verge of a nervous breakdown.

Alex made his way back outside. Resting both hands on his cane, he paused outside the tree. Huge slabs of concrete, piles of crumbled bricks, and slabs of wood lay all around. The people of the Conjurian were carting them away, brick by brick, stone by stone. The sounds of hammers and saws reverberated from the city streets.

Maybe magic would return to the Conjurian. Maybe not. Maybe they didn't need it. Alex was about to go on an expedition, not to find answers, but to see what answers found him. He limped across the field and headed back toward the theater.

EMMA

For the first time, Emma had somewhere she felt she belonged. And here she was, packing to leave it.

Her body stiff, Emma slung her bag over her good shoulder and left the dressing room in Derren's old theater, which had been her hospital for the past week. The hallway bustled with people, some with medical experience, many without, all doing what they could to help those on the mend. She tried to move as unobtrusively as possible, catching the whispers as she wove through the backstage area.

"That's her."

"She's the one who fought the Shadow Conjurer."

"And she fought off three Rag-O-Rocs too. Three!"

The warming glow of pride evaporated instantly as she remembered her victory in Plomboria. Those Rag-O-Rocs had been people too. Suddenly she didn't want to be recognized. Ducking her head, Emma walked out of the wings onto the stage.

"Miss Maskelyne!" Emma's doctor, surrounded by several other Jimjarians, all in white coats, hustled across the stage. "I do not think it wise for you to leave just yet. Please, back to your room. Your trip can wait."

"Hi, Dr. Arlo," said Emma. "I'm fine. Besides, you need the space."

Dr. Arlo grabbed Emma's wrist and checked her pulse. "It's always the ones who say they are fine who drop first. You're something of a national treasure. Dedi forbid something happen to you under my care."

"Doc, I'm okay." Emma took his hand in hers. "Thank you for all you've done. But I have to go. These people need you more than I do." She stepped around him, climbed down off the stage, and headed up an aisle.

"You be careful, Miss Maskelyne!" Dr. Arlo called after her.

Emma was grateful that so many of the Jimjarians and Conjurians had chosen to follow her and fight for her . . . but the attention was starting to get overwhelming. She was glad that it was time to sail off into the unknown.

As she entered the lobby and approached the doors, they flew open and another glass cylinder was wheeled in. Emma slipped aside under the balcony.

"I wish to speak with you" came a voice from the shadows behind her.

The man who stepped toward her no longer stood straight as a post. He was hunched, relying on his cane for support. Yet his eyes still sparkled.

Before Emma had known about the Conjurian, this man used to visit her uncle Mordo's house. Back then he usually made her want to hide in the grandfather clock or lock herself in the kitchen pantry. So Emma surprised herself when she said, "I was hoping to have time to speak to you too, before I left. Glad to see you're doing better."

Christopher Agglar tugged at his collar, which hung loosely around his neck. "Yes, well. Fortunately I was not entombed as long as some of the others."

"Did you know my parents faked their own deaths?" asked Emma.

"No. They kept it from me. In hindsight, that seems to have been the correct choice." His voice softened. "Given recent events, it would appear that my judgment and methods were lacking. It was only because of the Shadow Conjurer's pursuit of the Eye that I learned it had not perished along with your parents. I was willing to do whatever it took to retrieve it before he did. For that, I apologize. Please tell your brother that I apologize to him as well."

Was that moisture building in his eyes? Emma had thought Agglar didn't have tear ducts. Now she couldn't help but feel for him. "It's okay. I understand. You were doing what you thought was best for your people."

"Hmm," said Agglar. "Allow me to walk you out."

Agglar shuffled past her and held the lobby door open. "A new world requires new leadership. I believe Master Fallow is what the Conjurian needs now."

Emma nodded.

"There you are!" Rowlfin hopped up behind them. "I turn my tail for one moment to fetch you some soup and you vanish." The Jimjarian placed Agglar's hat on his head and supported him by the elbow. "Oh! Greetings, Miss Maskelyne."

"Hello, Mr. Fornesworth." Emma tried not to giggle, watching the formidable Christopher Agglar being treated as if he were a mischievous toddler. "Why can't anyone just call me Emma?"

"Sorry," said Rowlfin, stopping Agglar from removing the hat. "It will take some time to shake off the old formalities."

"Although it seems many have already been long forgotten." Agglar lifted the hat off his eyes. "Now, if it is acceptable to my nursemaid, I would like to see you off, Miss Maskelyne."

"Emma. Just call me—never mind." This time Emma did giggle as she followed the pair of them through the doors and out onto the street. They looked like an old comedy duo, Agglar slapping away Rowflin's hands as the Jimjarian tried to adjust his collar, only to have Rowlfin reach out a second later to straighten his master's hat.

Agglar was once more taking the hat off when Alex ducked around Gertie, parked right outside the theater. He stopped short at the sight of Agglar.

"Are you sure you packed enough stuff?" Emma tugged on the enormous bag slung over Alex's back.

"Planning for the unknown." Alex wobbled, trying to regain his balance. "Who knows what we'll come across?"

"You, Master Maskelyne, have everything you need right here." Agglar tapped Alex on his temple.

Alex looked from Rowlfin to Emma. "Okay, thanks. Got it."

"Have you seen Savachia?" asked Emma.

Alex looked as if he felt sorry for her. "No, Em. Haven't seen him once."

"Can't say I'm surprised," said Emma. But in truth she *was* surprised that Savachia had taken off without so much as a goodbye. Maybe he wasn't one for pleasantries—but she didn't think it was like him to forget a debt. And she owed him. She'd promised to let him have the Eye to see if it could help his mother.

Of course, the Eye wasn't any use right now, since no one—not even Alex—could figure out how to make it do anything. But if they could . . . well. She was sure that at that time she'd see Savachia again.

For right now she was enjoying the fresh air, which sent a refreshing spark through her. She looked past the Grubians' carriage, parked behind Gertie. The road that the carriage sat on dipped away down toward the docks. Scaffolding covered the buildings. Workers hauled carts full of supplies up, down, and across the street.

Leaning on his cane, Alex hobbled back over to Gertie, nearly toppling over from the weight on his back.

"You will, of course, bring her back in one piece," said Neil Grubian, climbing down from the carriage roof. He patted Gertie. Sternly, he said to Alex, "Take care of Gertie. She needs a good oil change and a greasing once a week. Keep her out of the cold, but make sure she doesn't get too warm. I labeled all her spare parts and—"

The mechanical alpaca butted Neil in the arm.

"Yes, yes," said Neil. "I'll miss you too."

The carriage rocked, and the door flew open. Pimawa, clad all in yellow, including yellow sleeves over his ears, tripped and caught hold of the doorframe before toppling to the ground. "Stairs. Have to remember to lower the stairs first," he muttered.

"What on earth are you wearing?" asked Alex.

Pimawa's covered ears twitched. "Pardon?"

"Oh, for—" Alex tugged one of the ear coverings off. "Why are you wearing a banana costume?"

"For your information," said Pimawa, offended, "this is traditional Jimjarian sailing attire."

"I'll stick with this," said Alex, tugging at his tattered sweatshirt.

"You look sharp, Pim," said Emma.

"Thank you, Emma," said Pimawa. "It cost me a few favors to get one in your size."

Emma's smile vanished. She glowered at Alex, who was

not trying very hard to smother a laugh. Pimawa's ears, one still covered in yellow fabric, drooped.

Rowlfin and Agglar had been watching from the roadside. Now Rowlfin, after making sure Agglar was stable on his feet, approached his son. His whiskers twitched and his furry brow was so furrowed it looked like tiny rolls of carpet stacked one on top of another. Rowlfin hugged Pimawa so tightly the yellow suit crackled.

"I am proud of you," said Rowlfin. "I wish your mother could see you." He held a startled Pimawa at arm's length. "You watch out for these two, you hear?"

"Of course, Father," said Pimawa. "I always have."

CHAPTER 18

EMMA

"Leaving without a proper farewell?" called a voice from behind Agglar.

Uncle Mordo's wheelchair did little to diminish his presence. He had lost thirty pounds, his face was sunken, and his ponytail had lost its sheen, but his eyes still commanded attention as he rolled between the kids and the carriage.

"You woke up!" said Emma. For a moment she felt as if she were back in the mansion where she'd grown up and Uncle Mordo had—once again—caught her doing something she shouldn't.

Uncle Mordo stifled a coughing fit.

"You shouldn't be out here," said Alex, worried. He hurried over to the wheelchair's side.

"No, he shouldn't!" Dr. Arlo stormed out of the theater and over to Mordo. "Is everyone going to walk out? Goodness, I shall have to lock down the theater."

"One moment, Doctor," said Uncle Mordo. "I am glad I came around when I did." He glared at the carriage.

Emma glanced anxiously at Alex. Was their uncle about to forbid this journey? If he did, what would she and Alex do?

Emma had been so joyful when she'd discovered that Uncle Mordo was not dead, as she and Pimawa and Alex had thought, but merely one of the Conjurians trapped inside Angel Xavier's glass cylinders. She and Alex were not alone in the world after all. They still had a family.

But did having a family mean they had to do whatever

their uncle said? For years and years, that was exactly what Emma had done. Now, though? After everything that had happened—did she still have to obey her uncle?

Alex looked as baffled as she felt.

"I expect you to listen to me," said Uncle Mordo, fixing them with a stern stare. "I am aware of what you both endured during my absence, but that in no way justifies—"

"Uncle Mordo," interrupted Alex.

"Let me finish," said Uncle Mordo. "I cannot allow you to go on this journey without a crew. I will put together a team of the finest, sturdiest sailors I know, and then—"

"Good point, but already taken care of." Savachia bounced out of the carriage, twirling a captain's hat. He extended his hand to Mordo. "A true pleasure to meet you, sir. I like your dress. I'm the crew."

"It's a kimono," growled Uncle Mordo.

"Wait, what?" said Emma, her jaw dropping in astonishment.

"Don't sweat it." Savachia winked at her. "We'll arm-wrestle to see who gets the beds."

"No," said Emma.

Savachia looked genuinely hurt. Emma didn't care.

"You can't vanish for a week, then show up and decide you're coming with us. You can't hustle your way in and out of people's lives when it suits you. Anyway, you can't just go off with us. Don't you have other people to worry about? What about your mother?"

"Where do you think I've been?" Savachia's eyes darkened. "There's nothing more I can do for her in the Flatworld.

If I'm going to find a cure, it'll be out there. Wherever it is, we're all going."

Emma still wasn't happy about the idea. Crossing her arms, she looked at Alex for backup.

"We could use his help," Alex said. Emma could hardly believe her ears. "Oh, come on, Em. He can think quickly on his feet, and he has a lot more street smarts than either of us."

Savachia grinned at his unexpected ally. Alex scowled back.

Emma gave up. "Fine," she said grumpily. "He can come. Because he might be useful. Not because I like him. Just so we're clear. Okay?" She stomped over to the carriage and tossed her bag inside. "Let's get going." She made sure she was facing away from Savachia when she smiled.

"Stop for one moment!" cried Uncle Mordo. "You have no idea where you are going or what's out there!"

"We're getting used to that." Emma surprised herself and her uncle by rushing back to his side and giving him a hug. "I'm sorry, Uncle Mordo. We have to go."

"We'll be fine," said Alex. "Madame Flarraj provided us with every map imaginable." Awkwardly, Alex leaned forward. He didn't look any more comfortable hugging his uncle than Emma had felt.

Mordo pulled him close. "I'm proud of you both." He released Alex, gripping him for a moment by his shoulders. "Your parents would be proud."

"We'll find them." Alex smiled at his uncle and then at Emma, who helped him up the steps into the carriage.

Emma climbed in after her brother. Savachia offered a hand to help her up, but she ignored him. With a shrug, he followed.

Pimawa was the last one up, retracting the stairs after him. He leaned out to close the door.

A spontaneous parade followed the carriage down to the docks. People waved and shouted from the scaffolding. Sawdust fluttered through the air like confetti.

Emma looked over at Alex, who sat in a beanbag chair with his nose brushing the journal Miss Harrafia had given them. Emma's chest felt lighter, knowing that after everything they had been through, some things hadn't changed.

She reached into her pack and pulled out the picture of her parents that Derren had given to her. They were onstage, rehearsing for a performance. Her mother leaned on the edge of a glass tank, soaking wet and grinning, while her father and Derren stood next to her, laughing.

They looked so lighthearted, so full of joy, so sure that nothing dreadful could ever happen to them.

She slid the picture between Alex's nose and the book. In the past, her brother would have ignored her, moved to a different room, and kept on studying. But now Alex closed the journal and placed it inside his bag, all the while staring at the photo.

Then Alex and his sister, at the same moment, lifted their eyes to the hatch overhead. They smiled at each other, and Emma stuffed the photo into her bag and climbed out. Alex followed.

At the end of the street ahead, they could glimpse the bright blue of the ocean.

"This should be fun," said Alex.

"There's a lot of definitions of fun," said Emma.

Alex waved to a group of bricklayers leaning over the top of a building. "We might discover a few more."

Without slowing, Gertie galloped down a boat ramp into the water, her legs folding into paddles.

Hundreds of Jimjarians and magicians, shovels and hammers still in hand, had gathered along a seawall to watch the launch. "A lot of pockets ripe for picking in that crowd," said Savachia, popping his head out of the hatch. "Too bad I'm stuck on this tugboat."

Emma glared over her shoulder at him.

"I'm kidding!" Savachia climbed the rest of the way onto the roof.

"Shouldn't you be swabbing the decks or something?" said Alex.

"I was a con man, not a pirate," said Savachia.

"We won't be needing those skills nor your comedic talents on this voyage, Master Sheridan." Pimawa joined them, trying without success to keep the map he held from slapping his face. Savachia and Emma helped him pin it down.

"Much appreciated," said Pimawa. "Based on what Alex has deciphered from your parents' notes, I mapped out the most prudent course." The wind tugged at the edges of the map, threatening to tear it. "However, it might be best to review it once we're all inside."

"We'll follow you," Alex said.

His words took Emma back to her uncle's mansion, to the last moment before she'd known that the Conjurian existed, that magic was real, and that she had a part to play in saving both of them. *Follow Pimawa!* Uncle Mordo had shouted before turning to face the Rag-O-Rocs and giving her and Alex time to flee.

And that was what they'd done. They'd followed Pimawa straight into a greater adventure than Emma could ever have imagined.

And it wasn't over yet. Emma helped Pimawa fold up the map. "That seems to have worked out so far," she said.

CHAPTER 19

Angel Xavier's head lolled to one side. On the rocky ground, he squinted up at the hooded figure as it stepped out of the hot sun into the cave where he lay.

"I'm so sorry. I'm sorry I failed you." Angel tried to push himself up against the cave wall. The moisture from his shallow breaths evaporated in the dry air.

"Easy. Don't get up. You did not fail." Derren removed his hood. He knelt down, examining the scorched vest strapped to Angel's chest. "Quite the contrary, my old friend. Things are going exactly to plan. Nevada is lovely this time of year."

Angel grimaced. "But I lost the Eye!"

Derren's smile iced over. "Precisely. Now *I* am in charge of the Conjurian and *I* have the Eye of Dedi."

"That wasn't the plan," said Angel hoarsely. "We were going to remake both worlds. A new world. Our world. That we'd rule together."

"Shhhh," said Derren, wiping a tear from Angel's eyes. "You're confused. I am to blame for that. I built you up into the greatest magician the Flatworld had ever witnessed. All that fame, the riches. It twisted your mind a bit, I'm afraid."

"Tear it down. Tear it all down. Create a new paradise for magicians. We were to be gods," Angel mumbled. He searched Derren's face for reassurance.

"Misdirection, my friend." Derren held the Eye in front of Angel. "The hand is not quicker than the eye. You of all people should have known that. It's all about audience management. Controlling what your spectators see and when they see it."

Burned skin bunched around Angel's eyes. "We were supposed to be partners!"

Derren sighed. "I was the one who invented the idea of a Shadow Conjurer to undermine faith in Agglar and the Circle. I was the one who convinced Henry and Evelynne Maskelyne to flee and leave the Eye behind. Of course, they never told me where they hid it. A small hitch in my plans. Nevertheless, I'm back on track. And yes, I was the one who made you into my puppet." Derren patted Angel's shoulder gently. "I must go. It is my turn on center stage." He stood up and moved to the mouth of the cave.

"I'll expose you!" screamed Angel. "Expose all your tricks! Your treachery! That'll be a show no one will forget!"

Derren turned. "You remember your first television special?"

"What? Yes." A wave of fear twisted Angel's face.

"You remember the illusion I wanted you to perform? You refused to do it. Walked off the set until I gave in."

Angel tried clawing his way toward the cave entrance. "No, no!"

"You were right." Derren pulled the hood over his head. "That illusion is much too dangerous." He walked out of the cave into the burning sunlight. Angel's cries echoed behind him. They were silenced as the cave entrance collapsed, sending a cloud of dust billowing out behind Derren.

Derren smiled. "The buried-alive trick always kills."

Exhaust grumbled from the convertible's chrome tailpipe. Hot air streamed over the windshield. Sand particles peppered Derren Fallow's sunglasses.

"Truly a remarkable machine, wouldn't you agree, Geller?"

Geller, swathed in a linen robe and wearing tiny sunglasses, scrunched his neck down. "Since there is no remotely interesting scenery to discuss, I shall agree with you, sir."

"It is not without its limitations," continued Derren. "Yet it is a mechanical wonder created to serve mankind." Derren stepped hard on the gas pedal; the car surged ahead. "Imagine the limits we could have surpassed if the Flatworld had never turned its back on magicians."

"Gracious, sir," said Geller in a drawl. "All these Flatworlders would have quit whining about the lack of flying cars decades ago."

"Exactly!" said Derren, slapping the steering wheel. "But that will soon change. So much is about to change. Aren't you ecstatic?"

"Simply frothing with excitement, sir."